THE MYSTERIOUS POINT OF DECEIT

A SEVERINE DUNOIR MYSTERY

BETH BYERS

SUMMARY

October 1925

Severine DuNoir has returned home and continued to investigate the death of her parents. She has, however, reached a roadblock. As she tries to break through, she comes across an unexpected offer of help.

While she delves into the history of her father's life, she also starts to investigate the haunting of an elderly woman. Just who is tormenting this woman and why?

PROLOGUE

*The soul is eternal, my darling, which is why kindness matters
so very much.
The love and kindness we give last just as long as the soul.*

—Sister Mary Chastity to Severine Euphrasia DuNoir

CHAPTER 1

OCTOBER 1925

NEW ORLEANS DUNOIR HOME

"What's all this?" Severine asked as she stepped into the parlor, her dog Anubis at her side. She'd been pulled from her office, where she had been slowly going through the contents of her deceased father's hidden office that she'd discovered at their countryside home.

Her great muscled protector eyed their invaders with the same disgust that Severine felt herself. She glanced out through the windows and saw the lovely day and the passing traffic. The New Orleans mansion had never stopped feeling suffocating, and she wasn't sure it could be more so at moments like these.

Her cousin, Florette, glanced up from the coffee tray

that had already been delivered. "Oh, I knew you'd want to see Mama and my brothers once they returned home."

Severine's gaze moved to the golden brothers. Henry and Barnabé grinned at her widely with perfect white teeth. Henry pushed back his too long blonde hair and his eyes raked over her. She could see the judgement and avarice and thought that men should try a little harder. Barnabé, on the other hand, ran his ringed fingers over his jaw and examined her chest before her face.

"Sevie," Henry said, stepping forward and kissing her cheek. He was followed by Barnabé, who escalated matters by kissing both of her cheeks while also squeezing her hands. "You grew up lovely."

"She hates being called Sevie," Florette announced, winking at Severine and then glancing towards her other brother. With the care of a true sister, Florette added with a hiss, "I told you that."

Severine stepped back and then crossed to the place near the fire where she could never not see her mother. This time, however, Florette's mother Delphine reclined there. She was another version of Florette. Blonde, lovely, bright and laughing. At one time, Delphine had been Severine's mother's very closest friend. It was through Delphine, in fact, that Severine's own mother had met her father.

In the months since Severine had returned to New Orleans, she hadn't seen her aunt, Florette's brothers, or Florette's father. The mother and sons had gone to the continent and Florette hadn't been well enough to leave with them. Her father had been in South America checking on some ranch there that poured in money—and trouble.

Severine hadn't regretted their absence and she

welcomed their return rather like she'd welcome an invasion of locusts.

"Auntie," Severine said, knowing Delphine hated the title as much Severine hated 'Sevie.'

"Sevie darling," Delphine said. "Look at you all grown up." Delphine rose with languid grace and moved her eyes over Severine from head to toe without approval. "What an interesting look."

"I told you she was so stylish," Florette said, not reading her mother's reaction correctly. "Severine has set a whole new style, Mama. I saw Adélaïde Broussard wearing a black dress and red lipstick the other day when she was failing to flirt with our Mr. Oliver. Adélaïde didn't pull it off nearly so well."

Florette blushed prettily. She'd caught the attention of their British acquaintance during a stay at the country house. The look she gave her mama said that she'd already waxed poetic and lengthy about Mr. Osiris Oliver and his friend, Grayson Thorne.

"Of course she didn't," Aunt Delphine said coolly. "Adélaïde is chubby and pink. She probably looked as if someone had died."

Henry scoffed and then asked, "Is this the fellow Grandmère believes has a wealth that rivals a timber baron? No one has wealth like that anymore. At least, no one except our Severine." His glance adjusted the 'our' to 'my.'

Severine didn't roll her eyes but she swore darkly that the day she turned herself and her fortune over to one of her avaricious cousins would be the day the gates of hell opened and freed their residents.

Florette's answer to her brother was, however, to roll her eyes and dart a disbelieving look at Severine all while fluttering prettily. Severine was surprised by a wince for Florette. The girl was half in love, and Severine wasn't sure that her feelings were reciprocated. Mr. Oliver, one of their two British friends, was indeed gallant and kind. She'd also witnessed him being gallant and kind to a good half dozen women in New Orleans.

"Florette tells me that one can often find Mr. Thorne and Mr. Oliver here," Aunt Delphine said, as though Severine had been whoring.

Severine shrugged. "At times."

"And often out and about," Aunt Delphine added with a narrowed glance inferring that was worse.

"They are indeed good friends of myself, Grandmère, Mr. Brand, and—"

Delphine scoffed at Mr. Brand's name. "That man has no place in this family."

Severine smiled serenely and crossed to the coffee tray that had been placed in the parlor while she'd been dressing. She poured herself a cup and sipped, ignoring her aunt's mild tirade, if a complaining fit could be both mild and full of rage.

"Technically," Barnabé said easily, "he's Severine's guardian." He put just enough emphasis on her name to show he had heard she didn't like the nickname.

Severine sipped her coffee again, suspecting the chicory-flavored café au lait might be all that saw her through the visit.

"When will Uncle return?" Severine asked to change the subject. She had no reason to respond to either Barnabé or Aunt Delphine.

"Soon," Delphine said with another cool smile. "He'll never forgive me if you're not living with us by then, darling. It's not quite the thing for a young woman barely 18 years old to live alone."

Sudden silence filled the room as the siblings turned from their teasing. Severine felt another ghostly swish of the past. Once upon a time, they'd fought together as children while Severine had lingered in a corner, silent and watching. Once upon a time, they hadn't been quite so interested in her. Once upon a time, she reminded herself, they'd all been spoiled children and not particularly fond of each other.

They were grown up now, weren't they? Tall, broad, handsome. Golden gods of New Orleans and wherever they went had ready smiles, handsome faces, and gazes that told a woman that she had enchanted them entirely. The gazes were, of course, lies, and they were, of course, rogues, but Severine thought women preferred pretty lies all too often.

"I'm afraid Uncle will have to be disappointed," Severine told her aunt easily. "Mr. Brand has taken the house across the street to look after me and keep an eye to propriety. I am quite happy here."

"No," Delphine told her flatly. "You'll be coming with us. I can't imagine what Alphonse has been thinking. This is what comes of being a widower. You've been shot, my dear. Your style is... unique, to say the least. It's entirely unacceptable for a young woman to become notorious. You can try this again when you're thirty."

Delphine meant, of course, that no one would marry Severine. She didn't bother to snort in disbelief. Delphine didn't think Severine would remain single either. Definitely not with her fortune. Nothing about Severine herself was appealing to Aunt Delphine and therefore, must not be appealing to anyone else.

Severine listened to a long list of reasons why she would be coming with Aunt Delphine and didn't bother to register a single one of them. When her aunt finished, Severine simply said, "Thank you for caring, Aunt Delphine. I am quite comfortable."

Barnabé laughed and told his mother, "Give it up, Mama. She's an independent woman. It's refreshing, really."

Severine didn't believe his approval was genuine any more than she believed the long looks that Henry was casting her way were real. Severine ignored her aunt's reply and rose, crossing to the window. The street was quiet enough when it wasn't Mardi Gras, but there seemed to be a strange auto lingering down the street. Was it someone who was keeping an eye on Severine?

She was sure she'd been followed in the last months since her brother had tried to make her appear mad and later tried to kill her. The attempt had failed, which was merely the opening act to having himself declared as her guardian rather than Mr. Brand. More specifically, the guardian and controller of all that money Severine's late father had amassed.

She glanced across the street and noticed that Mr. Brand's house was quiet. Was he inside working? Had he gone down to his office with his secretary and his assistant? Were his roommates, Mr. Oliver and Mr. Thorne, busy with their own investigations? She had yet to pull from them anything other than they were tracking someone who had disappeared into America and been traced to New Orleans.

Severine turned slowly back to her guests and she answered the question that had been hanging while her thoughts were elsewhere.

"Aunt Delphine," Severine lied, "I am listening. I am afraid, however, that I will be remaining here, in my father's house. I am quite used to being independent. I am also, as you know, quite reclusive. I'm afraid the bustle of your home would be overwhelming for me."

"She was, after all, raised by nuns, Mama." Henry glanced at Severine to ensure she knew he had defended her.

"Your mother would turn over in her grave knowing you were living like this," Delphine hissed.

"Oh Mama," Florette groaned. "Why—"

Severine lifted a brow and cut her cousin off. "Let's not pretend that my mother didn't find me generally disappointing in life. She'd never have expected anything different in the grave. Thank you for visiting, but I have an appointment that I must now prepare for."

Severine turned and left, Anubis at her heels. She bypassed the stairs and made her way to the kitchens where her roommate, companion, friend, and assistant, Lisette, was making bread with her mother.

Severine put on an apron, stepped up to the table and said, "I need to knead something."

One of the puppies barked once at her while Anubis crossed to the back door and stood nearby. Lisette's mother, Chantae, glanced up. "Did you leave the guests in there? I didn't hear the door."

"I did," Severine admitted. "I said I have an appointment."

"You do." Lisette laughed as Severine kneaded the bread dough like a master. "Later."

Severine smiled easily and then focused on the dough while Chantae went and rid them of Severine's family.

"Meline says you need new dresses," Lisette said as Severine started rolling out the dough for cinnamon buns.

Severine glanced up and nodded and then released her frustration on the dough. When she finished placing the cinnamon buns into a pan, she'd calmed down.

"I miss Sister Sophie," Severine admitted and then took up a plate of beignets and coffee to the table near the window. The dogs were chasing each other around the back garden and the birds were singing outside. She closed her eyes. "And the nunnery."

"Your problem is this house," Chantae said with the same flat honesty that Lisette had shown so many times. "It's haunted with your family."

"I don't want to forget them," Severine replied.

Chantae laughed harshly, but her tone was gentle when she said, "You won't. You don't forget your parents. Or what shaped you. You'll no more forget your mama than you will Sister Mary Chastity or the bread-making nun."

"Sophie," Severine said, rubbing her chest. What she would give for warm bread and tea with the sisters. Severine rose and let her dogs inside. Handsome Anubis crossed to her, sensing her melancholy, and put his head on her knees while she sipped her coffee. She set the cup down rather harshly. "I can't just live like this."

"You're right. You can't," Chantae said, glancing intently at her daughter at the same time.

"But I won't be what Delphine wants either."

"That would undo all the good your nuns did," Chantae agreed.

"Therefore," Severine said, "I'll do what they would want me to do."

CHAPTER 2

"What is this?" Severine asked as she looked over the accounts with Mr. Brand.

He looked at the entry on one of the pages and then, to her utter shock, his ears turned a deep, dark red.

"Ah—"

Severine glanced at Lisette, who was watching Mr. Brand with dark eyes that only intensified his blush. He cleared his throat and then coughed.

"It's something scandalous," Lisette whispered to Severine.

Severine looked at the entry that had only interested her in passing. It read: Mme. Thibodeaux, et al.

Lisette leaned over Severine's shoulder. She read it aloud. "Ohhh, Madame Thibodeaux."

Their gazes met. Lisette and Severine both had deep brown eyes like the shades of dark chocolate. Their gazes were filled with matching knowing.

"Mistress," Lisette and Severine said in unison.

"He must have loved her," Lisette told Severine, "given he saw to her after his death. Is her income guaranteed?"

Poor Mr. Brand with his heated cheeks. He nodded only once. He continued to avoid Severine's gaze, and she couldn't help but think back to her father. He hadn't been a kind man or a particularly loving one. He'd shown Severine dashes of affection, but he'd often been cruel to her mother. Severine sat so straight, a dowel of wood along her spine couldn't have made her more stiff.

"There are children." Mr. Brand's blush intensified painfully.

Lisette blew out, a long, dark sigh while Severine asked, "Are they all right?"

"They're fine. Madame Thibodeaux is a good woman. Kind and loving."

"They have what they need?"

He nodded and his gaze met hers. "Your father didn't want you to know."

She wasn't surprised. The heir didn't have to know about the byblows. She hated her father in that moment. "How many?"

Mr. Brand cleared his throat. "Three."

She nodded, taking in the fact that she had three more half-siblings. "Are there others? Beyond the Thibodeauxs? There are, aren't there?"

"A son. He's twenty-seven."

"He's all right?"

"Your father had already seen to him before he died. He was in school when it happened. He's since finished and is working as a doctor in Seattle, Washington. He never came back to Louisiana after he left for school."

Another older half-brother, Severine thought. She didn't know how she felt, but it wasn't emptiness. Anubis leaned against her leg and put his head on her knee, and she scratched his ears idly, giving herself a moment to think. An older brother who was wise enough to get away. Who'd chosen a profession that looked after others. She would assume he was one of the doctors who was kind rather than power mad, and she'd be proud of him.

"No others?" Lisette asked for Severine while taking hold of Severine's free hand. How lucky she was, Severine thought, to have Anubis on one side and Lisette on the other.

"There's one more son."

Severine waited.

"He's just nineteen. Your father left money for school and to get established in a career and home. He's supposed to go to Columbia University but hasn't gone yet."

Severine did the math and knew that just after his second son had been born and was still small and squalling, she'd come along and disappointed him with her sex. She bit down as Lisette made the right comments about how Columbia University was a good school, and he must be quite smart. How much more bitter Severine's arrival must have been then.

"No others save the ones we've discussed," Mr. Brand said. "The young Thibodeauxs and the other two."

"Boys?" Severine asked, thinking how her father would have been so bitter to have only one legitimate child and that child being a girl. It played in her head over and over again, and she knew she needed to let it go. She had felt love from him often enough, what little love he'd been capable of giving, but maybe he'd just saved the rest for those sons of his.

"Three girls. They're ten, eight, and seven."

Severine nodded, grateful that Mr. Brand and Lisette were aware that she was stumbling about in her head and carried on without her.

"What are their names?" Lisette asked.

"Elcie, Madeline, and Cosette."

Oh, little sisters. They looked like her in her imagination. Little silent waifs that blew into rooms uncalled for and disappeared without notice. Severine knew it was unlikely, but she felt this need to protect them and—given her own acknowledged half-brother had tried to kill her—the greatest act of love she could show them was to leave them be.

"Do they have enough to see them through this life, to settle them well?"

"They do." Mr. Brand's gaze was carefully fixed on Severine as though she were Lot's wife, just turned to salt. Would she blow away now? Severine wondered.

"Can she meet them?" Lisette asked for Severine.

Severine shook her head. "No."

"No?" Lisette asked gently.

"No. Not me. Keep an eye on them," she told Mr. Brand. "Make sure they have what they need. Some of what they want. Make sure if their mother has another lover, he's not unkind, but nothing beyond that."

"Oh Severine," Lisette said low and soft.

Severine sniffed as she said, "I think that's enough for today."

When she left the office, she felt a bit as though she should be changed by the knowledge of more siblings. Maybe she was, maybe she wasn't. Maybe she wished she were surprised. How lonely she'd been as a child. How she'd desperately wished for a sibling of her own. Back then, Andre hadn't counted, older half-brother and in her life though he was, he'd had no interest in her. She had thought that if she just had a brother or sister of her own someone would love her. Someone would care.

She needed to avoid them. If they didn't matter to her, they wouldn't matter to whoever was trying to hurt her.

Andre had, after all, tried to kill her. To steal her fortune and her life and then refused her offers to help him when they'd trapped him in his crimes. The only reason he was free today was because Grandmère had released him from the cellar, and he'd escaped.

She hated that she was as worried that they wouldn't like her. No, she thought, don't think those thoughts. Her mind drifted back to Andre. Where was he now? She laughed darkly, seeing Lisette's askance look and feeling Anubis as he leaned into her while they stood on the sidewalk. Andre certainly wasn't practicing medicine and caring for the ill.

"Life isn't fair," Severine said.

Lisette's scoff was timely and pointed. Severine found herself laughing. "Let's get the puppies and go for a walk?"

"I don't care to walk forever as you do," Lisette said and then elbowed Severine lightly. "Perhaps I don't mind this time since you've been forced to realize yet again that your father was a bit of a bastard. We have lunch with Meline first, however."

SEVERINE AND LISETTE met Meline at a crawfish house near the dress shop. It was one of the few in the city that didn't have the sign in the window reading, 'No blacks.' Severine and Lisette took a table near a window at the front and ordered for Meline, so she could use her break time to eat while they chatted.

Just after their food arrived, Meline rushed over from the dress shop and shoved a pile of drawings at Severine before digging into her food. Severine flipped through the drawings, pausing on a sketch of herself in a long slinky dress that dipped low in the front and the back.

"My scar will show." Her brother had shot her earlier that summer and the mark was still red and angry, though healed over. It announced its existence with the contrast of red against ghostly white skin.

"Humans have scars," Meline told Severine easily. "Whoever you spend your time with is going to want to see it anyway. I've heard spoiled ladies talk about Andre a few times while they're buying dresses. Usually lamenting that he was so handsome and wondering whether he'd still be considered a good catch. Those fools are going to be looking for the scar so you might as well let them see it and then look down your nose at them."

Severine gasped. She ran one finger down her nose while she asked, "Surely, no one would want to marry someone who tried to commit murder?"

Lisette leaned back, unsurprised. "If there's one thing I've learned, it's that women will look over a lot to not be the old maid."

Severine's mouth dropped. "Attempted murder?"

"They don't believe it was an attempt at murder. Your grandmother is putting it around that it was an accident and you're high-strung," Meline told Severine flatly. Her dark brown eyes moved over Severine, and she added, "I thought you knew."

Severine wasn't even surprised. Surprised or upset. If

anything, she was upset that she hadn't realized. "Thank you for telling me."

"She's not upset?" Meline asked Lisette. "If that were my granny, I'd throw a fit that would ring in her ears for a decade!"

"She knows what the woman is," Lisette said. "No love lost there on either side."

"Have you seen her since…everything?" Meline asked low.

"At events where we overlap," Severine answered. "We smile and press cheeks."

Meline scoffed and then gestured at the drawings again, watching carefully as Severine moved through the dresses. The first dress had made her lift her brow, but she'd wanted it right away. Despite the scar, she'd wanted that long slinky thing.

The next drawing, however, had Severine lifting both brows and dropping her jaw the tiniest bit. It was Severine in a suit. The black pants were loose and flowing, but they were matched with a white version of a man's shirt, a black tie, black suspenders, a vest, and a coat. It looked a bit like someone had combined the flow of beach pajamas with a gentlemen's suit. Despite the austere black, it was completely feminine.

The men's white shirt was pleated down the front. A man could have worn it, but it would still skew feminine on Severine. The black tie was embroidered, black-on-black, with dragons and roses. The vest had matching embroidery.

"Oh." Severine's head tilted. "I like the shirt especially. I'd want a good half-dozen of those in white. The high collar, all of it. And the black ties. How about, along with these pants, a few skirts as well? Something to go with the jacket and the tie? Like what a school girl would wear, but a bit longer?"

Lisette looked over Severine's shoulder and her mouth dropped too. She gasped and then her eyes narrowed with an evil smirk. "Please wear that for the first time with your grandmother. If I've ever seen anything that will cause an old Southern woman's hair to curl and knock her into a swoon, it's that ensemble, cher."

Meline nodded and Severine kept looking. There were also designs of sporting clothes in only black and white. No colorful tweeds for her. Everything, really, was black with shades of white, wine red, and deep purple as accents.

"I set some things aside for you at the shop," Meline said. "If you want, I can send them over. You can keep what you want, and Madam will bill you for what you keep."

Severine nodded, immediately agreeable. Just the act of sending them to Severine would put Meline in a good position with the shop owner, and Meline had an excellent grasp of what Severine might actually wear.

"Madam is desperate to know who is making your clothes. She'd murder me if she realized it was me, and I'd be out of a job for sure." Meline's mouth twisted with a grin. "Ah well."

"Ah well," Severine echoed with a matching grin. "I have a party coming up that Grayson and Oliver are determined to attend. There's been some activity in the house and the Spirit Society wishes to investigate and see what they can find. It's also with a woman who knew my father quite well according to rumors."

"So something startling then," Meline nodded.

"Eye-catching," Lisette told Meline. "Her aunt is determined to reel Severine into line. She needs something that refuses to be contained."

"A queen's dress, something commanding and independent." Meline nodded. "But appropriate for a spooky ghost party."

Severine didn't have the imagination for dresses the same way Meline did, and Severine needed the visuals of the drawings to have an idea of what Meline could imagine up in moments.

They finished eating and Severine approved the wardrobe Meline had been working on. Then they parted ways. Lisette left to write notes for her, and Severine found her way to the city park with the three dogs to walk, as Lisette called it, endlessly.

The day rolled by as Severine wandered the park. She fed birds and sat under a tree and read one of the books she'd taken from her father's hidden library. She reviewed her list of questions about her father and mother and their lives. She walked more.

The melancholy was fading in the face of her true emotions. She felt as though she were treading water and getting nowhere. She'd read all the reports of her father's business, and her conclusion had been that they were well-told lies. The problem was that whatever Father had been up to during the Great War, he'd ended afterwards.

By the time he'd bought the big house in the country, his business practices had changed. Which wasn't to say that the business partners hadn't delved immediately into running booze into the country and secretly manufacturing deep in the bayou.

She started to read her list again when she felt eyes fixated on her. How long had he been staring? How long had it taken for her to become aware? She met those familiar eyes across the park, and then her brother lifted his hat to her, finger shooting her like a child playing cowboys.

She pretended she wasn't bothered, and then she stayed longer because she wasn't going to be driven away from a place she loved by a man who should be begging her forgiveness.

CHAPTER 3

Severine and Lisette walked out of the house, leaving behind the dogs, to Anubis's distress. He was too well behaved to express himself beyond flopping to the ground by the door and huffing darkly. Kali and Persephone, however, flopped down next to Anubis and whimpered.

"Here we go again," Lisette muttered. "What do you think? Will we finally discover what Grayson and Oliver are up to?"

"No," Severine said quietly as Mr. Brand stepped out of the vehicle and opened the back door for them. He had purchased a secondary car for her, this one a chauffeured Rolls-Royce for moments like these. The driver was a friend of a friend of Lisette's mother, and he could be counted on to keep an eye out for Andre and as backup if things turned sideways for Severine again.

The house they were going to was outside of the French Quarter and had a large old mansion with a good amount of land. It had the requisite carved pillars, arches above the windows, thick velvet drapes, and even the stone lions of the very rich. Severine kept herself from rolling her eyes at the stone lions. In her opinion, lions should only attend a castle. The smaller the house, the smaller the cat. In fact, she thought, she should really get a set of carved house cats for the walk up to her house.

Severine took Mr. Brand's hand and let him guide her out of the car. He turned to Lisette and then they all looked up to see Mr. Thorne and Mr. Oliver waiting for them. They'd become allies, of a sort, in the hunt for the killer of Severine's parents. For them, it was opportunities like this event that Severine provided them. They had provided her their wits, strength, and eyes when she'd needed them. Those things had been valuable, she reminded herself.

Grayson Thorne held out his arm.

"You look ravishing," he told her.

She smiled a thank you. The dress that Meline designed was a black sleeveless number with no back. The top half of the dress clung to her form while the bottom half ended in waves of fabric that trailed on the ground. There was a black lace wrap lined with wine red to provide the sheerest touch of color, outside of her wine red lipstick. The final touch was the gloves that reached several inches past her elbow.

Severine placed her gloved hand on the crook of his elbow and let him lead her up the steps. At the top, she saw Grandmère accompanied by Andre. Grayson stiffened as Severine faced her brother.

"Grandmère," Severine said easily, her eyes moving with contempt over both of them. "You'll be glad to hear that only Andre's income has been stopped, but of course, if he had tried to collect it, Mr. Brand might call in the authorities."

"You are a terrible sister," Grandmère hissed low, her eyes narrowed. "Appearances must be preserved."

"Mmm," Severine agreed as easily as before, but this time she laughed. She rubbed her shoulder lightly.

"You should cover that thing."

"But then the young women of New Orleans might think Andre is a catch. Beau of the ball and all of that, dear Grandmère. One should be publicly minded first." Severine eyed her brother coldly and then said, "The trust has been amended. Obviously, you've been removed. We were able to change who inherits for me as well."

She smiled at them and turned away as Grandmère demanded who Severine's heir was.

"You're not of legal age," Andre hissed at her.

"Yes, but things can be done all the same. Also my father never trusted you, so he put some clever wording into the trust and the way it will be administered. It is sad to be you and it seems, quite poor as well. Maybe murder your father instead, since you have a chance in hell of ending up with a little something there."

"You don't know what you're doing," he said, grabbing her arm. Grayson Thorne reached out and pulled Andre away in a manner that had him yelping and immediately letting go.

"You'll have to teach me that," Severine said and then continued through the grand hall.

MRS. THEODOSIA GRANTLEY WAS ANCIENT. She was the kind of old that was frail, curled, and heavily wrinkled.

Her thin white hair barely covered her scalp from what Severine could tell, but Mrs. Grantley had covered it mostly with a turban. Her dress was as black as Severine's, and she too wore a slash of powerful red lipstick.

Under all of that age, Mrs. Grantley's eyes were sharp as ever. Her gaze moved over Severine and then Mrs. Grantley stepped back as if she needed a little distance for a proper look. With the lack of care of a woman who is past social niceties, she said, "You look nothing like your mother."

A girl tittered, giving herself away for eavesdropping. Mrs. Grantley examined the girl, with—was that an edge of disgust?

Severine blinked just once and then said, "I'm aware."

"That's hardly a bad thing," Mrs. Grantley added. "Your mother was another daisy just like Clementine over there. A dime a dozen and of little lasting interest. I suspect you have far more depth." Mrs. Grantley snorted and then reached out and gently touched Severine's shoulder. "Is this where he shot you?"

Severine's head tilted.

"I'm well aware of what you have in Solange Charpentier. I don't believe your grandmother's lies about what occurred, and anyone who knows her well knows she's colored the story for her own wants."

"That is where I was shot," Severine answered, refusing to speak about her grandmère.

"Grandmama," a woman said. "Why don't you come sit?"

They all turned and Severine found herself looking at a face she somewhat recognized. "Amelia?"

"Sevie," Amelia replied. She wasn't happy to see Severine, but there was no animosity in her expression.

"Come Grandmama, I'll get you some champagne, shall I?"

"No," Mrs. Grantley said. "I'm not dead yet and there's time enough to sit in a corner." Her eyes moved back to Severine, and she asked, "Was the nunnery they shut you away in haunted?"

Severine paused, considering her answer. "It's difficult to say."

"What does that mean?" Mrs. Grantley demanded. "Do you believe in ghosts?"

"I believe in life after death. I believe it's possible that we could see the dead. But I don't believe that the dead linger in a house to haunt a person when there are, probably, so many more things to do. So, do I believe that the nunnery is haunted? No."

"But you have a reason to say you believe in ghosts?"

Severine fiddled with her finger before she answered, "I suppose I do."

"Your parents?"

Severine shook her head. Did she believe her mother or father would somehow push their way through the veil of the living and dead to convey pride and love for her? No, she didn't. Not at all. But, should the day arrive that others she loved died, Severine wouldn't be surprised to see them one last time.

"I have never seen a ghost." It was an equivocation, and she could see that Mrs. Grantley wasn't impressed.

"Then why?" Mrs. Grantley shot out. "Why do you believe? Most are skeptics."

Severine glanced at Mr. Thorne, who had never said why he was part of the Spirit Society. She looked behind her at Mr. Brand, who had never said one way or the other. Next was Lisette, who said things were better left alone. Mr. Oliver, like Mr. Thorne, had never expressed his true feelings.

Severine turned back to Mrs. Grantley. "I've only loved a few people truly and deeply. And I have only trusted those few. One of them had an experience, and I completely trust that person."

"You've never felt as though you've been haunted?"

Severine paused again before answering. "I have felt that often, but I'm not sure I believe it is ghosts. Rather it feels like memories with too much weight."

Mrs. Grantley patted Severine on the face, ignoring the audience of the offended eavesdropper Clementine, her own granddaughter, and Severine's friends. At further distance were Grandmère and Andre, and all of them were watching Severine with the matriarch.

"I believe," Mrs. Grantley told Severine. "I have always believed and though I've never seen a thing, I have often felt as though my Roscoe or my parents were nearby. Do you feel as though your parents are nearby?"

"I don't know," Severine replied, deciding that only stark honesty would do for this woman. Mrs. Grantley had an air about her that pulled more and more truth from Severine.

"You're a good girl," Mrs. Grantley said and then as if it were comforting—though it was not—she added, "Your parents were fools."

Severine leaned down and kissed the air near Mrs. Grantley to avoid leaving lipstick on her and then said, "And you are kind. Thank you for inviting us to your party."

"Perhaps," Mrs. Grantley said, "after today you'll believe."

An excited expression crossed Mrs. Grantley's face

and then she welcomed the rest of them. As they moved away, Mrs. Grantley told Grayson, "You look like her, you know."

Grayson went from languid to tense, and Severine admitted to herself that her ears perked up.

"She's very like you. Those green eyes, that fox's jawline, that air of a certain something. Self-possession, arrogance, and cleverness all wrapped into a very pretty little package."

Grayson cleared his throat, but there was still the smallest of quakes in it when he asked, "When did you see her?"

Mrs. Grantley shrugged and glanced at her daughter, but if Amelia knew who they were talking about, she said nothing.

"Please," Grayson added, and Severine thought it might have been the first time he'd said that word for more than a refill on his coffee. "Please think?"

Mrs. Grantley's brow furrowed. "I'm really not sure."

Oliver cut into the conversation. "We need to know."

There was too much snap in Mr. Oliver's tone for Amelia. "Come Grandmama. You should relax."

The dark look Amelia Grantley gave Mr. Oliver had him backing up, but there was a stubbornness in his jaw only matched by Grayson Thorne.

"What was all that?" Lisette demanded the moment they stepped into the parlor with the low light and the flickering candles. "Sister?"

"Never mind," Grayson muttered.

Lisette's jaw dropped and her gaze narrowed on Grayson and Oliver, but Mr. Brand was the one who said, "I thought we were allies here. You're looking for a person, and we didn't even know it. What's happening?"

"That doesn't give you the right to all of the details of our lives," Mr. Oliver told the others flatly. He turned and walked away.

Grayson Thorne looked after him, glanced at the rest, his gaze pausing on Severine for a long moment before he too excused himself and left.

"What in the world was that?" Mr. Brand asked, rubbing his brow.

"She's obviously their reason," Severine said with a deep breath. "She, and whatever happened to her, are their secrets."

"They were awfully intense about when she was last seen," Lisette said. "But—"

"Why wouldn't they tell us she was missing?" Mr. Brand muttered. "What is going on?"

"It's interesting that they found their way to our family," Severine added, with a cold logic that left her colder as she spoke. "Why were they hanging on Grandmère when we first arrived? Remember how they were dancing in attendance at that first party, Lisette?"

She nodded, her frown as deep as the one that Severine was hiding. "Mr. Oliver has spent a lot of time with Florette, but he's never done or said anything that would be considered a promise."

"He was furious in the way of someone who is afraid for a person they care about," Mr. Brand said. "I know that feeling with you, Sev. But perhaps not as a brother."

"What do we know about them really?" Lisette demanded with a hurt that also matched Severine's.

"We know that they helped us at the big house," Severine replied. "Grandmère must have invited them because she thought, when it came down to it, they'd be eyes and mouths for her. Only they haven't been."

Mr. Brand cursed low and then apologized before he added, "Can we trust them?"

The silence was too long for comfort. Severine finally said, "We're the fore-swearers if we change the agreement now."

Lisette groaned. "And to think I liked them."

Severine paused, her mind racing. "They've never lied to us. They've been reliable for our part. We knew they were here for their own purposes. Having those purposes be secret or painful doesn't make them our enemies."

"But can we trust them?" Mr. Brand asked.

Severine glanced after Mr. Thorne and knew in that moment her feelings had become more complicated than she had known. She also knew she was partially ready to deal with those feelings regardless of what they might someday find out about Thorne and Oliver. Perhaps there was no need for concern. But, perhaps there was very much a reason for concern. Either way, Severine's heart was still recovering from a lifetime of hurt, and she didn't trust it in the least.

CHAPTER 4

She saw it first when she rose to avoid Grandmère. Osiris Oliver and Grayson Thorne were aware enough of Severine that when she turned towards the large French windows and then lingered for too long, Mr. Thorne stepped up next to her.

"I—" He paused, watching what she watched. "Is that—"

Severine glanced up, realizing she felt a flash of fury followed by a determination to put up a wall between them. She had trusted him too quickly. She tried not to fixate on his square jaw and those dark green eyes or the handsome face. Handsome meant nothing, she told herself. What mattered was trust, but it had been shattered so easily, and now it was gone.

Careful to keep her tone even, she said, "I believe someone is wandering through the trees out there."

"You don't think it's a ghost?"

"I think that doctored wine has been passed around, that we're surrounded by those who want to believe in something, and that there's a woman in black in the trees just after enough time has passed for the wine additions to be effective."

Severine smiled politely but coolly as she eyed Mr. Thorne, and she could see he saw the shift in her. It was as if he didn't blame her for the change, and he wasn't apologetic. Whatever force had brought Mr. Thorne to leave his home country and journey here wasn't something he was going to share easily, and she wasn't sure she could move past it given that he'd somehow worked out of her so many of her own secrets and worries.

She shook her head and turned, motioning to Mr. Brand, who joined them at the window.

"What the devil is this?" he asked.

"I believe," Severine said, "this is where we cry out and motion everyone over."

"Whatever do you mean?" Mr. Brand asked.

She winked as she said low, "I'll show you."

"Show?" Mr. Thorne asked. He examined Severine as though she were something of a puzzle to him, but she sidestepped when he offered an elbow.

With forced loudness and a touch of pretend fear, she cried out, "Oh goodness, Mr. Brand! What is that?"

Heads turned their way, and she felt his hand on her arm as she leaned towards the window and gasped in a pretense of horror. She gasped for real as the figure darted into the trees again, seeming to disappear. It wasn't fear that caused that second gasp, but wonder. How had they arranged such a thing?

Severine, however, had little doubt that this whole scenario was intended. Why did these people have a Spirit Society when so much of it seemed intentionally set up? The first Ouija board session she'd attended had been followed by more than one where she'd have bet her fortune was pre-arranged.

They'd had their tarot cards read, but the fortune teller had known too many specificities to be believed. It wasn't the vague and yet somehow too accurate generalizations. Instead, the woman had used actual first names and references to private past events.

Severine had also seen members of the society murmur together in corners unbothered by the supposed supernatural in front of them, and her suspicion had grown to certainty that this society had a purpose far beyond the named one.

A crowd formed around the window, straining to look out. She took that moment to slip back away and watched from behind as excitement flooded the group, even while Amelia Grantley rubbed her arms and stepped back. Severine eyed Amelia, who watched carefully with an interested expression, but without pushing forward.

She felt a hand on her arm and glanced up, finding Mr. Brand.

"Are you well, Severine?" Mr. Brand asked. "You're not afraid?"

As her guardian, he had become her protector since she'd left the nunnery. As her protector and the only person who seemed to care what she wanted or how she felt, he'd become the brother of her heart.

"That," Severine said in a low whisper, "is a woman dressed in black with something over her face."

"You don't believe it is a spirit?"

Severine snorted, trying to hide her mocking given the excited chatter only a few feet away. "I lived in a nunnery, Mr. Brand. That isn't so different from the sight of Sister Bernadette coming home late and her face covered from the cold. I believe the only difference is that someone made an effort to use wispier, black, lacy garments rather than a habit. Outside of those differences, the only thing that I see is that our actress is staying in the shadows, no doubt purposefully. Are you a believer, Mr. Brand?"

"No, rather not. I fear that this wouldn't have been my passion if not for our quest. I'd much rather spend an evening with a book and a cigar or the company of good friends."

The quest to uncover her father and mother's killer was her focus, and therefore Mr. Brand's efforts, not a desire to prove there was life on the other side or to reconnect with a dead loved one. If she were entirely honest with herself, Severine didn't want to connect with her dead parents.

She wanted justice for them. She wanted to know why they had died, but she didn't need to see them or speak to them again in this life.

That 'why' haunted her. Why had they been murdered? If someone was going to kill Father, why Mother too? Was she only an accident of circumstance? Or had Mother been the intended victim all along? Was it Father's business interests? Did Mother have a jealous lover? Had they committed a crime that had begged for vengeance?

Severine had spent the last several months pursuing the truth and being blocked by those who knew the details of her parents' lives. Was it because they were attempting chivalry with the arrogance of a Southern gentlemen who was so certain he knew what was best for her?

Or, perhaps, it was because they were criminals looking to remain undiscovered. Severine smiled at her friend and then glanced beyond him to Lisette, who had gasped as dramatically as any of the true devotees of the Spirit Society. Lisette winked at Severine and nestled in close to Mrs. Grantley. She held out a steadying arm, and the old woman took it tightly.

They whispered together while the entire crowd murmured. Mr. Oliver had weaseled his way near Mrs. Grantley, no doubt pursuing the aside she'd made about Mr. Thorne's sibling, but Mrs. Grantley hushed them.

Severine glanced at Mr. Thorne, who had stepped back to lean down to Amelia Grantley and listen intently to her murmur. A moment later there was a sound in the hall, and Amelia gasped. "But the servants have been let go for the night. We should be alone!"

A near-stampede to the hall followed, and when the door was open someone cried out, "The stairs!"

Severine, given her height and the vantage point at the back of the crowd, saw the dark form in the shadows of the stairs. The guests chased after, and the form looked back and then seemed to fade away.

Severine lifted a brow when Mr. Oliver called back, "There's no one here."

She wanted to roll her eyes and call out, "Check the closets, my good lad," but she said nothing, choosing to watch instead. She wasn't surprised that Mr. Thorne and Mr. Brand were doing the same.

There were mostly young devotees that Severine guessed were true chasers of spirits and the supernatural. The older crowd, those of her parents' age and her aunts and uncles, hadn't presented themselves. Why? Why was Mrs. Grantley the sole representative of her age beyond her friend, Mr. Harland Ruggles? He was one of those Southern gentlemen who spoke in a slow drawl, was prone to smoothing his rather dominant white mustache, and was known for pretty words. Severine had come to the conclusion by their second meeting that he practiced his compliments. She had also concluded that he knew far more about her father than he would ever tell her.

He had, in fact, told her not to worry herself over it. He'd actually squeezed her hand, and she wouldn't have been surprised if he'd patted the top of her head. Thankfully, they were both spared the indignity of such a thing, but he had told her to smile more and suggested she try wearing a pretty pink gown to attract the boys.

Mr. Ruggles had sent Severine flowers the day after he'd told her not to worry over her parents and to count her blessings. Severine had wanted to shout at the fellow, but instead she'd forced a smile and told him she was blighted by stubbornness.

As the crowd of excited spirit-chasers gathered to discuss what had occurred, Severine frowned at Mr. Ruggles, who, for once, wasn't telling her what to do or leaning over some other woman with that frustrating slow drawl and uttering pretty words that meant nothing. Instead, he had a dark frown and it was fixed on Mr. Oliver. Severine's head tilted and she scolded herself even as she crossed to Mr. Ruggles and asked, low and sweet, "Mr. Ruggles, I wonder if you might lend me your ear and your advice?"

He started at her touch, but he smiled down at her the moment she said the magical word 'advice.'

"Of course, my dear," he said, patting her hand on his elbow. "Of course. I could do nothing else. Your father was a friend of mine, you know. We shared business interests, friends, this passion, and of course, so many other things. I could do nothing less for dear Lukas."

Severine let her gaze move slowly to Mr. Oliver, and then she winced dramatically before she turned her eyes wide and pleading up to Mr. Ruggles.

"Dear Mr. Ruggles—" Severine used her sweetest tone. "—I don't know if you're aware, but Grandmère introduced myself and my cousin, Florette, to the gentlemen Mr. Oliver and Mr. Thorne." Mr. Ruggles waited, but she could see him filling in the holes as he wanted to. "What do you know of them?"

Mr. Ruggles's head cocked and he said, "You know, I don't approve of these foreigners. It's not so bad when they're Brits like those two. But what are they doing here?"

"I believe Mr. Thorne's grandmother lived in the area," Severine said. "So I suppose he's a little Southern."

"Yes, yes." Mr. Ruggles nodded sagely and then added, "Knew her, I did. Genevieve Braxton Thorne. Good woman. Good family."

Severine made a mental note, but she knew she wouldn't forget the name.

"Genny," he continued, reminiscing. "We were children together, did you know? She was the belle of all the balls. Quite the catch with all that money behind her."

Severine waited, breathlessly forcing herself to lean into him, so she seemed an attentive bird. She couldn't transform herself into her cousin, Florette, who would—certainly—be preferable to herself, but Severine could at least try to channel her cousin's mannerisms.

"Sweet, pretty Genny. I dreamed of marrying her."

Severine pretended to be entranced by the romance of it, but the pretty manners of Mr. Ruggles hadn't extended —even once—to anything other than a gilded cage for the women in his life.

"Where did she live?"

"Oh, an old mansion quite near yours, I recall," Mr. Ruggles mused and then nodded. "Yes, yes. The red brick one a few down from yours."

"Did they sell it?"

"I don't believe so." Mr. Ruggles shook his head. "But it's one of those things. Quite a center of otherworldly activity." He laughed mockingly and then grinned condescendingly at the group of women searching for the 'ghost' up the stairs. "I'm surprised Mr. Thorne hasn't had the Society over there."

"No one wants to live there?"

Mr. Ruggles shook his head again. "A whole terrifying drama, I'm afraid, my dear. Better to avoid the location than to be sucked in yourself."

Severine paused and asked, "Is the house to do with what happened to his sister?"

"Mrs. Oliver?" Mr. Ruggles lifted his brows and then winced. "Bad business that. Bad business, indeed, my dear. Better to stay out of it."

CHAPTER 5

*M*rs. Oliver? Severine's gaze moved to Mr. Thorne and from him to Mr. Oliver, who was the steady hand at the side of Mrs. Grantley at the head of the stairs. If Mr. Oliver was married, why had Grandmère tossed Florette at the man?

"My dear Severine," Mr. Ruggles said, focusing on her in that annoying way of his, "you shouldn't wear so much black. You look like a ghost yourself. You aren't going to catch a man that way."

Severine lost control of her tongue long enough to laugh. "I think we'll all find that the money my father left me is more than sufficient to catch me a whole slew of men regardless of the color of my dress."

His gaze widened and he demanded, "But you want to make your husband happy."

"I suppose," Severine added, "when I meet the man, should I love him, I may want that very much. But do you know something?"

He waited, and she paused long enough to make it dramatic before she continued. "I haven't met him yet, so it may well be that he likes black dresses on women. Or he doesn't care. Perhaps he'll care more for my mind than my looks. After all, youth doesn't last. So, I shall endeavor to hope for a man who appreciates the other things I have to offer beyond my money and whatever attractions I may possess physically."

Mr. Ruggles laughed a little mockingly. "You'll find your man is stepping out on you if you don't try a little harder than that."

Severine's gaze narrowed upon Mr. Ruggles. "Well, if so, I'll find I have chosen a man with no honor and, therefore, chosen quite poorly."

Mr. Ruggles's expression mocked her, but she had little patience for him once he'd stopped speaking of Mrs. Oliver.

Instead, Severine excused herself and crossed to Grandmère. Her brother was attempting to charm some young heiress who seemed quite immersed in the conversation, and in the distraction Severine stated, "You know Mr. Oliver is married."

"Was married, my dear. Widowers are the best of husbands. They know the pain of losing once and are more careful with the second bride." Grandmère lifted a mocking brow. "How did you know? Been listening at keyholes?"

Rather than snapping back, Severine asked, "Why is it such a secret?"

"What?" Grandmère's lip curled just enough to signal she was utterly certain of what the secret was and why it was a secret.

"Does Florette know that Mr. Oliver was married?"

"I believe that the fact he was married makes him all the more desirable."

"Because he's in so much love with his wife that he won't speak of her?"

Grandmère's laugh was enough to have Severine wincing for herself. Was she wrong? Was Mr. Oliver not happily wed? Why were they looking into what happened to her if she wasn't beloved? Severine's gaze narrowed on her grandmother. "Is his wife dead?"

Grandmère's mean smile was enough to make Severine doubt herself. "I thought you were friends with the man."

"Florette is quite fond of him," Severine told her grandmother. "Surely you care about that. Do you want her heartbroken?"

"She'll be fine. She's a good girl."

"Good girls have hearts," Severine snapped.

"Good girls do as they're told."

"So you think, even though you aren't really her grandmother, you can tell her to marry a man who is obsessed with his dead wife?"

"I think Mr. Thorne and his sister were born flush with money. The kind of wealth your father had. I think that his sister married Mr. Oliver regardless of his own financial status, and he's got a fortune because of that."

Severine's gaze narrowed on her grandmother. "So, Florette will be there when Mr. Oliver finally lets go of whatever he's pursuing with his wife."

"He's pursuing the truth of her death," Grandmère replied casually. "He wants a body or a witness to have her declared dead. Once she is, he'll find that he's led Florette on and that a good girl has given him her heart along with her patience. He's too honorable not to marry Florette and then she will have a fortune that will see her through this life."

Severine didn't have it in her to answer. Instead she turned away. Grandmère was a nightmare.

Before she could get away, Grandmère's claws dug into Severine's skin. "You stay out of it, girl."

Severine would do no such thing. Instead, she yanked her arm free and crossed to Mr. Brand. "They're looking for a sign of what happened to Mrs. Oliver."

Mr. Brand started, and his eyes held the same shock as her own.

"Mrs. Oliver?" It took him only a breath to make the same connections she had. "Do they believe she's dead?"

Severine shook her head helplessly. She had no idea what Mr. Thorne and Mr. Oliver thought about what had happened to Thorne's sister and Oliver's wife.

There was another scream up the stairs and someone shouted.

"It's outside again!"

"It's moved through the walls!"

An unholy scream followed that Severine couldn't decide was from the audience or the ghost. Either way, it caused a rash of gooseflesh that had her rubbing her arms. She didn't even believe this was anything more than an act, but it was affecting her.

The form seemed to move through the walls, and the crowd rushed to see if they could see it come through the wall, throwing open the windows and leaning out.

Severine crossed with Mr. Brand to a window and saw the same form as before. A woman, all dressed in black, clinging to the shadows as she moved smoothly, disappearing and reappearing in the trees.

"Look!" a man cried.

"It does seem like she's floating," Mr. Brand muttered with disbelief.

Severine didn't believe it and she was searching for a reason as to how it could happen. A moment later, she felt cold air moving across her, and she frowned deeply, deciding to ignore it rather than let herself get caught up in the fervor. "Perhaps someone hired a ballerina or some sort of dancer."

"You don't think it's real?" a stern voice demanded behind them.

Severine and Mr. Brand both gasped with an actual start.

It was Mrs. Grantley, her old face fixed in fierce determination on Severine. "What do you think it is?"

"A living woman dressed in black who is clinging to the shadows."

"Surely that could be a ghost," Mrs. Grantley said with a sniff. "How did she get through the walls."

"Perhaps," Severine agreed. "But I can't quite believe it, and I'm sure we can both think of ways about how this might have been done."

"Why?" Mrs. Grantley demanded almost as though it were an accusation. "Why would anyone do that to me?"

Carefully, Severine considered before she answered. "I—"

Mr. Brand interrupted. "Miss DuNoir has a great deal of experience with women wearing black outfits in otherwise spooky environments, Mrs. Grantley. For our Miss DuNoir—well, she's seen quite a few women walking under the trees in the dark, all in black."

Mrs. Grantley examined Severine and then the old woman sighed. "That's what I think too. There's been so much playing at spirits and the supernatural among the society that it's impossible to believe anything anymore."

"I'm not sure we're supposed to have the answers the true seekers in the society are seeking, Mrs. Grantley." Severine's voice was low and kind, and she hoped it was gentle enough for the woman who seemed desperate to get the answer she was seeking.

"There have been episodes," Mrs. Grantley told Severine and Mr. Brand. "Things that I can't explain, but I can't quite believe."

Severine wasn't sure how to respond to such a thing and she glanced at Mr. Brand to get his take.

"Don't look at each other," Mrs. Grantley snapped. "I'm old. I'm dying even, but I'm not senile."

Severine winced. "I didn't think you were."

"Don't lie to me."

"Mrs. Grantley," Severine retorted, giving the woman her irritation, because Mrs. Grantley didn't want to be coddled. "I was taken in by nuns. I have seen them become senile, and I've also seen them stay sharper and cleverer than me into their old age. You aren't confused. You recognized me as a grown woman after all these years, and you've never struggled with my name...so yes, if you tell me that something is happening in your home, I believe you."

"But you don't believe it's ghosts."

Severine searched the woman's face and knew Mrs. Grantley wanted the truth. "No, I don't. That wouldn't be my first suspicion."

Mrs. Grantley sighed and Mr. Brand reached out and took her hand. There was such sweetness in the move that

Severine wished she could see him as something other than a brother.

"This"—Mrs. Grantley gestured to the people gathering back into the parlor—"was never supposed to be the joke it has become." Her tears shone and Severine could see real and fervent passion in Mrs. Grantley's gaze. "It's been fun over the years, but now that I'm at the end, I remember that earnest desire to learn something more, to reach beyond, to see and know and be unafraid. It's been my greatest passion since my dear husband died. To know what happened to him."

Severine's breath caught on one of Mrs. Grantley's words. Unafraid. Oh goodness. She'd seen too many people die. Sister Léonie dying on a cold evening in late February from illness. She struggled for breath up to the end, but she hadn't been afraid when her eyes turned sightless and empty. Sister Charlotte had been confused often in the years before her death. Severine had spent many a day with Charlotte when she was still mobile so she didn't get lost. When the time had come, Charlotte murmured a name, smiled, and a breath later, she was gone.

And then there were her parents, lying upon one another soaked in blood.

Severine dug her fingers into Mr. Brand's arm as she struggled with the weight of her empathy for Mrs. Grantley. It took a thick swallow and a careful controlling of her voice as she said, "I don't think that there is anything to fear, ma'am."

"You haven't lived my life," Mrs. Grantley told Severine flatly. "You were raised by horrible parents, I agree. I never liked your father, and even though he was the greater crook, he was better than that fool Flora. You, however, were handed off to nuns. Who can feel sympathy for you? You have the aura of peace of a woman who has done no great wrongs. Of course you don't fear the next life. Your lack of fear doesn't apply to all of us."

Mr. Brand glanced down at Severine, and she could see the agreement in his gaze. "She doesn't see it in us. She's young yet."

"What?" Severine asked.

"The weight of all of our mistakes," Mr. Brand told her. "They're so heavy if you have any bit of a soul."

Severine wasn't sure she agreed. She saw the mistakes, or if not the mistakes, the way they weighed down the people around her. But, she didn't think that they deserved the weight they carried. She thought that some-times people punished themselves for far longer than they deserved.

"Have you changed?" She spoke to Mr. Brand, but the question was directed at both of them.

"I try."

"There are some things you can't take back," Mrs. Grantley told Severine starkly. "There are mistakes that you can't fix. There are things you did—that you knew were wrong—and there isn't a way to go back and fix them."

Severine didn't have an answer for that, so she just said, "Maybe I haven't made the big mistakes yet."

Mrs. Grantley snorted.

"But I have known those who have."

Mrs. Grantley eyed Severine with thick doubt.

Severine laughed. "We all think of nuns as women who felt a call to the Lord and were always good and sweet and perfect, but they aren't. They have varied histories and often things behind them that would fell weaker souls. Peace is possible, Mrs. Grantley."

Mrs. Grantley shook her head and Severine knew that there wouldn't be any convincing her.

"Do you think you're being haunted?"

"Yes," Mrs. Grantley answered with exhaustion. "But as much as I want to believe that it is my dear Antoine or my mama, I think it's something else. My fear, my dear, is that it is those I've wronged rather than those who might love me still."

Severine really didn't know what to say to that. "You think you are being haunted, but not by your husband? A vengeful haunting?"

"If, however, your theory that this is a living person playing with my heart is the correct one"—Mrs. Grantley closed her eyes with a fragility that spoke of the death she was so sure was coming—"I should like to know."

Mr. Brand cleared his throat and Mrs. Grantley's eyes opened, her gaze sharp and fixed. She studied Severine before she spoke. "I know things about your father. Things that will help you with what you are trying to find out."

Severine held her breath. Was this it? Was this the break she needed to finally start moving on why her parents had been killed?

"I'll tell you everything I know about them."

Severine cursed herself slightly even as she knew she had to add the rest. "And Mrs. Oliver?"

"And Mrs. Oliver," Mrs. Grantley agreed, "if you find out who is haunting my house."

Severine glanced at Mr. Brand, who shrugged and

then she acknowledged she couldn't do anything else. "Of course, we'll do whatever we can."

"I should have said I'd help you without bargaining," Mrs. Grantley told Severine.

She laughed lightly and then told the woman kindly, "I should have said the same."

CHAPTER 6

Severine was dressing when Lisette's mother, Chantae, knocked on the door.

"Cher," Chantae said with a careful gentleness. "Are you well?"

"I saw my brother again," Severine told the woman, who sat next to her on the edge of the bed. She curled into Chantae's side and felt the warm weight of her arm around her shoulders. It was almost as good as curling into Sister Mary Chastity's arms. Her nose pressed into Chantae's shoulder.

"He wasn't a good brother before, cher," Chantae said in a low murmur.

"But now he can never be," Severine whispered. "I'll never get a good mama like you, a father who wasn't wicked, or a brother who hasn't tried to kill me."

Chantae smoothed back Severine's hair and said with common sense and her usual flat honesty, "It was never a very likely chance."

Severine laughed an unhappy little sound. "Sister

Mary Chastity would tell me to count my blessings, look for opportunities for kindness, and put my brother from my mind."

"Vengeance is mine," Chantae quoted with the same ease as any of the nuns.

Severine sniffed and sat up. "Thank you."

"You're my girl now, too, cher," Chantae told Severine. "You rescued Lisette from pinches, cruelty, and poor wages. You rescued me from cleaning those houses, and set me up over the house where my girl lives."

"I dragged her into my troubles and asked her to follow me into madness," Severine said and then rose, crossing to her closet.

It was somewhat amusing to open the door and see all of her black and grey dresses. Anything else would look and feel awkward on her. Was it because she'd embraced the look since Meline had created it for her? Or was it because Severine had spent the last six years in a nunnery? Maybe it was because she felt as though she were in mourning for the parents who had been buried years ago, but she wasn't able to let go of their deaths. There were too many unanswered questions about their murder that her mind couldn't ignore.

Now that she'd been pursuing it for a while, she felt as though her continued existence required the solution. Would her half-attempt save her life if she stopped? Severine didn't think so. She felt hunted by the very hounds of hell, and she didn't think her great guard dog, Anubis, would be enough protection.

With a random decision, she grabbed a dress.

"No," Chantae said, crossing to the closet and taking out another dress. It was a straight black dress that was sleeveless and dropped into a pleated skirt below Severine's hips. She wasn't overly curvy, but her dresses normally left her somewhat feminine. This one hid her chest and her hips and left her a long line of lean.

With her slightly curling hair hovering around her shoulders and back, and with a little blush on her cheeks and a little color on her lips, she was still undoubtedly feminine. She added a long strand of pearls which she looped around her neck a few times.

When she was finished, she looked put together enough that Chantae nodded in approval.

"That Meline is a genius. You'd look like a wilting flower in a rose color."

Severine laughed and followed Chantae down the stairs. As they reached the bottom and turned towards the breakfast room, there was a knock at the door. Severine glanced at Chantae, who lifted a brow. They had seen those silhouettes through the frosted glass before. On the other side of the door were Mr. Oliver and Mr. Thorne.

Severine wished she'd decided how she felt about their secrets. She was in the same indecision as she'd been the night before. On the one hand, she felt they had every right to their secrets, and she'd known they were here in search for someone. It was just that it had never come up before, and she'd assumed it didn't matter as much as her own concerns. Which was, when she got down to it, arrogant and idiotic. She didn't like facing that truth about herself.

At the same time, she was self-doubting enough to wonder why they had insinuated themselves with her. Was it really the sister? If it was, why had they never talked about her? What if, instead, they were being pushed into approaching Severine? What if they weren't allies at all but another set of gentlemen in the command of the same fellow who had controlled her brother?

Was she being paranoid? Or had she been too trusting this whole time?

Severine crossed to open the door while Chantae disappeared, saying something about cafe au lait and beignets. Slowly, she swung the door back and eyed the gentlemen.

They were, in some ways, opposites. Osiris Oliver was golden with blue eyes and a skin that lent itself towards flushing without being overtly fair. On the other hand, Mr. Grayson Thorne was dark. His hair was even blacker than Severine's.

They were both tall and both clearly strong. They had the kind of energetic awareness that said they were comfortable in their skin and very capable. They had the attitude of those who could strike out at any moment but stayed on the side of the line without aggression.

Mr. Thorne's intelligent, green eyes fixed on Severine, and she refused to look away. She wasn't going to pretend she had the same faith in them she'd had before. "Good morning."

In the days before, Severine might have simply opened the door and allowed them entry. This time, however, she waited, poised with the door in hand.

Mr. Oliver looked at Mr. Thorne when the moment had lasted too long, and he said, "We've news."

She started to tell him to wait, that she wanted Mr. Brand present, but her guardian opened the door to the house opposite hers and jogged across the street. "Sever-ine, good morning."

She stepped back and let them inside, but not without

catching the look that Oliver tossed Thorne. "We were about to have breakfast," she told them.

Severine led the way to the dining room and avoided the powdered sugar beignets for plain ones given her black dress. Lisette joined them a moment later, and by the time they'd all received food and coffee, an awkward silence had fallen.

"Well," Lisette said, glancing at Severine and then smiling as her mother joined them. "Momma and I would like to know why we haven't heard of your sister before."

"It's private," Mr. Oliver answered quickly before Mr. Thorne could reply.

"So are the things Severine has been investigating."

Mr. Oliver's jaw tightened. "They're not the same thing."

"Aren't they?" Lisette shot back while Severine idly sipped her coffee, ready to observe the battle rather than to participate herself. She took a deep breath when Oliver barely held back a curse.

"There are a few things, I think," Mr. Brand said calmly, "that have made this a larger concern. I think that the first is why."

"Why?" Mr. Thorne asked. "Like we said, this is a private matter."

"That's not what I mean," Mr. Brand replied in that same calm manner. He'd have been a good priest, Severine thought, with that steady tone and easy manner. It belied the mind and the stubbornness behind his straightforward expression. "What I meant was that I think we're all a little more concerned about the motives behind those who insert themselves into Severine's life now."

Mr. Thorne looked shocked. "So you think we're involved with this mysterious person who manipulated

Andre into hurting Severine?" Thorne's gaze moved to Severine. "Is that what you think?"

She wanted to say no. In fact she wanted to say a lot of things, but what she said was, "There are grounds for concern on our parts outside of a better understanding of what is driving your own quest."

"What's that?" Mr. Oliver snapped. His cheeks were ruddy, and she had little doubt it was because of his fury.

"In the simplest of terms, Mr. Oliver, you have been insinuating yourself into my cousin's life and heart, and I think you know it." Before he could object, she held up her hand. "It doesn't make it better, sir, if you insinuate yourself into the hearts of a half-dozen young women. Florette only knows what you do to her, and I cannot and will not watch as you break her heart while you pursue your wife."

Mr. Oliver's mouth snapped shut, and the ruddiness of his cheeks morphed to a mottled purple. He did not, however, bother to lie to them.

"Perhaps," Mr. Thorne inserted, "we can take a deep breath and all calm down. We might have reasons for concern among ourselves, but we also have a history of relying upon each other."

"I think," Severine said, "that my own worries about who might be trying to slip into my life will leave me cursed with paranoia that may follow me beyond these events. I should not like to feel this way, always. You did help me, Mr. Thorne, at the big house. Your presence along with Mr. Brand's kept me from the asylum my brother hoped for and the grave as an alternative. I haven't forgotten that, and neither have the rest of us."

Mr. Thorne pushed aside his untouched beignets. "I

can only tell you that we're not under the manipulation of anyone else."

Severine nodded once, though her heart railed at her. Could she trust him? Should she trust him? If she couldn't trust him, however, maybe she couldn't trust Mr. Brand or Lisette or Chantae. She didn't want to live like that, so she said, "All right."

She glanced at Mr. Brand, who nodded as well, but she recognized the look in his eyes. It told her that he wasn't worried about the state of his soul after this, but about her. She had little doubt he'd use whatever connections he had to look further into Thorne and Oliver regardless of what they decided here today.

So, Severine leaned back and made the choice to take them into her confidence. "Mrs. Grantley believes that someone is purposefully haunting her. She is offering, for our help, information about your sister and my parents."

Mr. Thorne's eyes widened. "Mr. Oliver was—"

"Romancing the little blonde, Clementine, tonight? Pursing his own agenda with the girl?" Lisette said without an edge of forgiveness.

Mr. Oliver's purple mottled face had faded back to red and started to escalate again when Mr. Thorne said, "Yes. She told him that she didn't understand why her parents were even involved in the Spirit Society. They mocked it at home."

Severine lifted a brow, searching her mind. "Clementine is her name, right? Isn't she a Claremont? That's her family name, I believe."

"Indeed," Mr. Thorne replied.

"They were founders," Severine told them. "The Claremonts. We knew that some of the members of the society are no more believers than our Mr. Brand, but why would they mock it as founders?" She ran her fingers along her jaw as she considered and then lifted her pearls, fiddling with the shape against her jawline.

"It occurs to me," Mr. Brand added, "that we have met some of the pre-eminent members of New Orleans society in the Spirit Society socials, but Lisette was also welcomed without a blink by anyone other than your grandmother. No offense, Lisette."

"None taken, cher," she replied. "Don't think I hadn't noticed. There was that jazz singer a few weeks ago. At the party at that big mansion near the bayou."

"There was a priest at the one before. With the walk through the cities of the dead and the stories from the cathedral."

Mr. Oliver had calmed down once the talk had turned from him and his romancing of Severine's cousin. He rubbed his brow and muttered, "We met the mayor at one of these."

"The governor too," Mr. Thorne added. He cursed low. "Anyone could be involved."

"They all are," Severine said. "The Spirit Society is a place for those of all statuses—and with things to offer— to meet. It brings together the powerful among the religious, the political, and those in business worlds, but also those less powerful who might still be in their presence. You are as likely to rub elbows with a future president as you are to be speaking to the man who grows half the tobacco in the South or the man who baptized his children."

"It narrows nothing," Thorne murmured.

"They're snakes," Severine told the rest of the table. "We just need persistence and a steady eye, and they'll turn on each other. Just like they did to my father. And, I assume, whoever can account for your missing wife."

Mr. Oliver caught the message. The firm word, the harsh look, the lifted brow. Severine wouldn't cover for him. Not when it came to Florette. Not even though he'd given her no promises. Florette was the ideal, innocent, sweet young thing, and Severine wouldn't watch that lively little spirit be crushed by any man when Severine could help stop it.

CHAPTER 7

"Iwonder," Severine said after Mr. Thorne and Mr. Oliver left, "if we should think more deeply about what we've learned. I wonder, in fact, if it couldn't help the snakes turn on each other."

Before she could explain, there was another ringing of the doorbell and in a few moments, Chantae returned and said, "That woman, Mrs. Grantley, has arrived. She'd like to talk to you."

Severine glanced at Lisette and Mr. Brand, and they all rose, leaving the table with the remnants of beignets and empty coffee cups and a few shreds of the trust that had been built between themselves and their British friends. The trust wasn't gone entirely, but it would take time, Severine thought. Time and awareness to consider upon what they really felt.

For Thorne and Oliver, Severine was willing to admit to a level of trust and a desire to trust them. For Mrs. Grantley, however, the same could not be said. They seated themselves in the parlor and asked for a coffee tray for their guest.

The dogs had followed silently. The girls had gone from small puppies to nearly the size of Anubis. The three hounds had been compared to hell hounds by a good dozen people during their walks, and their names, Anubis, Kali, and Persephone, only lent to the impression.

As they waited for the coffee, they talked about Amelia Grantley, who was single but had hopes in one of the lads Severine had met and forgotten almost immediately. They talked of Mrs. Grantley's other four grandchildren who varied in ages between seventeen and still at school to twenty-five and quite handsome. That was said with a lingering glance after taking in the French Quarter mansion that Severine lived in. Severine chose to ignore the inference.

"You've abandoned my request?" Mrs. Grantley finally said.

Severine shook her head.

"Young people, like yourself, have no understanding of what it is like to be an old woman, alone and friendless. I'm not surprised. Your mother was thoughtless and entirely without feeling as well."

"Why do you think someone is haunting you?" Severine asked, the moment after that comment and having no desire to explain her gut reaction to Mrs. Grantley in general. It had, Severine noted, been on the edge of nauseating. She would follow that instinct without fail. "Why would anyone haunt you?"

"Because I'm an old woman?" Mrs. Grantley laughed coldly. "That means I've had quite a lot more time to develop a long line of enemies behind me, dear."

The dear had been condescending, and Severine didn't

react. Mrs. Grantley had taken a turn from last night, taking on an offended high-handed manner that made Severine regret their bargain.

"There must be another reason," said Mr. Brand. "I am guessing that you've been part of the decades-long play-acting of hauntings that the Spirit Society indulges in. Handing out wine before a ghost walk does beget issues and I'm sure there have been many."

"Knowing how to fake a haunting…well…" Lisette said and trailed off purposefully.

"Yes, obviously," Mrs. Grantley. "Hiring actors and charlatans. Unseen noises and thumps with ropes and pulleys. The sudden cold spots. It's not the first time someone thought of buying and hiding dry ice. It adds to the overall effect both with the gas that comes off of it and the cold in the air."

Severine waited as Mrs. Grantley mumbled to herself. "The slamming doors when no one is supposed to be there. The sounds of murmuring. I'm an old woman. You can make creaking noises outside of my room and call my name, and it's not like I can chase them down. It's just… it's…not what I would have expected from my enemies."

Severine sipped her coffee to give herself time to consider.

Lisette, however, wasn't so gentle. "What do you expect from your enemies?"

Mrs. Grantley laughed coldly and Severine flinched. She'd lived with women from their early twenties to their nineties for the last half dozen years. In all that time, she'd seen those wrinkled faces convey a variety of deep feelings. Love, longing, regret, fear, hatred, but never had she seen this sort of evil twist to an expression. It brought to mind the discussion the night before of regrets and guilt and Severine realized that Mrs. Grantley must have more than her fair share of both. Or, perhaps, not enough.

"A knife in the back? A painful poison? Something agonizing."

Severine wished she could feel for the woman. Only, on the other side of the guilt was a slew of people that Mrs. Grantley had hurt. People whose lives had been affected by her actions. People who might have lost money, homes, loves—Mrs. Grantley's guilt was so deep, it could have been anything.

Rather than providing a false comfort, Severine focused on the mundane. "Who are your heirs?"

Mrs. Grantley snorted, but her face softened slightly. "Much of what I have was directed by my husband already to my sons. I have some money, however, to leave to my grandchildren, which is what I have done. Left equally between the five of them. Why they would try to haunt me for it, I don't know. All of them know I would give them the money if they needed it."

"Perhaps there is someone who doesn't hate you enough to murder you but hates you enough to torture you," Lisette suggested.

Mrs. Grantley scoffed.

"Why are you part of the Spirit Society?" Severine asked.

Mrs. Grantley rubbed her brow and then set her coffee aside. "It's all mixed up. It was an earnest thing for me and Genny."

"Genny?" Mr. Brand straightened. "Genevieve Thorne?"

Mrs. Grantley lifted a brow. "Mmm. Yes. Mr. Thorne's grandmother. I knew her when she was Genevieve Braxton. I visited her in London where she lived with her husband. Joined her at their version of believers pursuing the supernatural. It had been a club for decades. Genny and I had told each other so many times how New Orleans needed one. When I came back, I talked to a few other believers about it, and we started more earnestly."

"How did it become a place where people conducted secret business?" Lisette asked with confidence that declared it a truth rather than a theory.

"Oh early days," Mrs. Grantley answered, confirming the truth. "It wasn't uncommon for my husband to take over all the things I was interested in. He was a controlling man, involved in everything I did. Everyone I knew. Everywhere I went."

"It sounds horrible," Severine told Mrs. Grantley, but she didn't think the woman felt the same.

"If he were a monster—" Mrs. Grantley laughed and then admitted, "He could be a monster. But I always did what he wanted, and so he wasn't a monster to me. An occasional fist, a few days in the bedroom. He could have been worse."

In her mind, Severine repeated the, 'It sounds horrible.'

"No thank you," Lisette muttered.

"You modern girls don't calculate beyond your independence. There's more to marriage than that, dear. Though you'll be lucky to find anyone decent, considering your—" She raked her eyes over Lisette's face and body and didn't finish with the color of her skin.

Severine gasped but Mr. Brand snapped, "That's enough of that, Mrs. Grantley."

Mrs. Grantley seemed shocked, but her mocking laugh told what she thought of their reaction to the unspoken insult to Lisette.

"Lisette is a valuable member of our household," Severine said, "and from what I can see, your marriage has little to recommend other than a gilded, and sometimes painful, cage."

Mrs. Grantley's mockery didn't fade. "Lisette's mother might know something about the value of never having to worry about being hungry. Never having to worry if your children will have clothes and food. Antoine was all that I needed him to be. If he was too rough at times, he was never too poor."

"She knows those things well," Lisette told Mrs. Grantley, "but I think she'd rather know those things than whatever you're feeling right now."

"What happened to your husband?" Mr. Brand asked when Mrs. Grantley crossed her arms over her chest and scowled at all of them.

"He…" Mrs. Grantley sniffed and then set her coffee cup back down with a sharp click, "…died."

"That sounds like there's more to the story," Severine said, striving for how Mr. Brand sometimes spoke to her. Sort of gentle and calm and probing all at once.

"He died." Mrs. Grantley looked to the side, focusing on the corner of the room. "He was out. He seemed fine before he died. He collapsed."

"A heart attack?" Severine asked, but she could see Mrs. Grantley didn't think so herself.

"He's from a long-lived line. The kind who turns out old codgers who die in their beds irascible and irritated after a century. He wasn't that old. He wasn't…I don't know."

Again that sideways look. Again that focusing in the corner.

"If you want our help," Severine told the woman flatly,

leaving out the gentleness, "you'll be straightforward with us."

"You want my help too," Mrs. Grantley said as if she had all the cards.

"Yes," Severine replied. "But we're not dying and you are not our only hope. How can we even trust you?"

Mr. Brand—with that calm, gentle tone—said, "I fear I must insist upon some proof that you can help us."

"Both us," Lisette inserted, "and Mr. Thorne and Mr. Oliver."

Mrs. Grantley's gaze narrowed but she finally offered what might have been news of interest if they hadn't already suspected. "Your guess about the other purposes of the Spirit Society are correct."

"We had figured that out for ourselves," Mr. Brand replied.

She paused and then continued as if he hadn't spoken. "They use some of the charlatans they hire to pass information, letters, even money. It's so easy, you know, for anyone present to come up to the performer and speak to them. Entirely unsuspicious."

"Do you know who Andre was working for?" Lisette demanded.

Mrs. Grantley lifted a brow and her slow smile made one think she knew just that. What she said was, "That information is worth far more than a simple payoff. Madame Cocotte, our theatrical fortune teller and society charlatan, can be bought by anyone."

"What does that mean?" Mr. Brand asked. "The society charlatan?"

"Ask her who hires her. She's been used to provide the desired ambiance. They also use her to pass messages and the like. For a price, she'll probably tell you things you might want to know. She has been performing for the Spirit Society for quite some time."

"When my parents were alive?" Severine demanded.

Mrs. Grantley smiled smugly.

"Why do you think your husband was murdered?" Lisette demanded. "Do you think the person who murdered him is the person who is tormenting you?"

"I'm quite sure it is not."

"Why?" Mr. Brand asked.

"I have felt, for some time, that my son, Philip, murdered my husband."

The words tolled like a death bell and the rest of them were struck silent.

Lisette recovered first. "Why?"

Mrs. Grantley sniffed, but this time there was feeling behind it. Her eyes were shining when she said, "Antoine never was without his flask. Never except for when his body was brought home."

They all waited, knowing that wasn't the end of the story.

"After I realized it was gone, I mentioned it and Philip chided me for borrowing trouble as though the missing flask meant nothing. I knew, however, it was gone. I wondered at it. I had wanted to follow my husband's wishes to give it to our other son, and it wasn't there."

"And then?" Lisette asked with that flat command that required honesty.

"And then I saw him returning it. He denied he did, but I saw it. He did it late. The door between my room and Antoine's room was open. It was open, and my son crept inside, turned on the dressing room light, shuffled about, and then left. He didn't live with us, you know. I asked the butler the next day if Philip had come, and it was clear he had. I told him to keep it between us as a favor for me."

"The butler agreed."

"He knows better than to disagree," Mrs. Grantley said simply.

"So the flask was back?" Severine reached out and petted one of the puppies while Anubis leaned into her side.

"It was back, it was empty, and it had been cleaned."

"What did you do?"

"I asked Philip if he knew anything about it."

"He said no?" Mr. Brand asked.

"He said no," Mrs. Grantley agreed. "Then I gave it to him and told him I knew his father would have wanted him to have it." She laughed meanly. "It's good for Philip to carry the reminder of what he did. Antoine of course, wanted Antoine Junior to have it, but sometimes a wife has to sidestep the wants of her husband."

Severine eyed Mr. Brand and Lisette, who both seemed to have reached the same conclusion. They were quite done with Mrs. Grantley and yet, they knew they couldn't be.

"What about Mr. Thorne's sister? What happened to her?"

"All I can give them is a name," Mrs. Grantley said, "and I'll be saving that until this is through."

Severine glanced at Mr. Brand and Lisette. They weren't going to get anything more of use. Lisette rose. "I'll see you out, ma'am."

Lisette enjoyed ending the interview with the woman, and Severine couldn't help but hide a smile. She didn't blame Lisette a bit for that move as they all needed a long walk to cleanse their palettes after that woman left. The moment the door closed behind her, they sighed in unison.

"What a woman," Mr. Brand said with disgust.

"What a mess," Lisette added.

"What to do next?" Severine asked and none of them had an answer.

They eyed each other and then threw out ideas until they'd decided upon hiring someone to follow Mrs. Grantley and her grandchildren along with someone to watch her house.

CHAPTER 8

"I've found her," Lisette crowed two days later.

Severine glanced up from her dressing table where she was applying lipstick as Lisette repeated, "I've found her."

"Her?"

"Madame Cocotte." Lisette's smirk was so self-satisfied, Severine had to laugh. It was ill-timed, and she smeared her lipstick. She muttered low as she carefully dabbed off the lipstick, refreshed her powder, and then carefully reapplied her lipstick and then grinned in the mirror at Lisette.

"How did you find her?" Severine turned to face her friend and noticed the gleam of triumph in Lisette's dark brown eyes.

"Sleuthing, brilliance, and persistence," Lisette said, holding cupped hands over her head and moving them back and forth.

"And?" Severine prompted.

"And," Lisette grinned cheerily, "perhaps I might have

known a girl who provides fortunes down in the French Quarter."

"Perhaps?" Severine smirked and then rose. "Do I look appropriately grim enough?"

"You look like a nun transfigured into a bright young thing and got stuck halfway there," Lisette told Severine. "Except, it looks intentional and fabulous."

"I suppose that's what I am," Severine admitted as she straightened her skirt and then added a hair band to her long black hair. It hovered around her shoulders and down her back. Her dress was sleeveless and her white shoulders peeked through the long black hair. "Stuck halfway between my time at the nunnery when my only thoughts were fixed on my parents and now. If only I could find who killed them, I might be able to do something else. Be something else."

"What would you be?" Lisette asked curiously. She had little sympathy for Severine as far as being fixated on her parents' death. They had, both of them, hard childhoods. Severine, however, had never wanted for food, shelter, or even safety. Lisette had struggled for all of those things, but she'd been wrapped in love from her mother and grandmother.

"I don't know. Perhaps I'd be an adventuress." Severine chuckled at the idea. "Could you see me in trousers and a white men's shirt with a kerchief around my neck?"

Lisette rolled her eyes. "The only sort of adventuring you'd be doing is horrifically long walks along moors and among the heather like Heathcliff from Wuthering Heights."

Severine paused and hated herself for a moment for asking, "Have you read Wuthering Heights?"

"Surprised?"

"Only with a large dash of embarrassment for wondering about it at all."

Lisette snorted. "I read it only recently. Took it from your library here. It was all in tatters."

"I read that one over and over again before my parents died." Severine shuddered at the memory. "It seemed as though only Heathcliff and Catherine felt as I felt."

Lisette choked on a laugh.

"Yes, I know," Severine muttered, "I was ridiculous." After a moment, she added, "I'm sorry it was surprising to me."

"It shouldn't be," Lisette told her flatly. "It wasn't like I went to a good school, thick with books in the library."

Severine reached out and took her hand. "Your native genius has shone through all the same."

"That Heathcliff—I'm not a fan. But I went for another, and there isn't more?"

"Try the other Brontë sisters." Severine rubbed the back of her neck and added, "I always felt quite linked to Jane Eyre as well, and she has survived my childhood while I find myself quite disgusted by the residents of Wuthering Heights."

Severine grinned and then whispered, "Sister Bernadette read novels. She kept them hidden under her bed in the cell. She was utterly serious about plants and studies and research, but she dabbled in novels which was quite disapproved of by the nuns, you know."

"Oooh, a rebellious nun," Lisette mocked. "What else did she do? Drink a second glass of wine at dinner? Sleep late?"

"Stop it," Severine said easily. "They loved me when no one else did, and Sister Bernadette shared her novels and her plant knowledge."

"So you can grow tomatoes? I like them fried and green," Lisette joked.

"Poisons, silly. Didn't I ever tell you she grew poisons and medicines? Tinctures and the like?"

"Poisons!" Lisette paused. "There's a sun room at the back of the house. You should start your own. You'll never know when you need a good poison, cher."

"One that can be traced to me? I think it's rather like a loaded gun, dear Lisette. It's too easy to use if it's right there. A little sprinkle in Grandmère's coffee, and my life gets surprisingly easier. What if, instead, we find the killers and then discover Paris?"

"Paris?" Lisette's eyes brightened and she pretended to consider, then mockingly checked her calendar.

"Paris, a swing by the nunnery, maybe a little trip through Prague."

"Prague?" Lisette groaned. "They didn't teach Prague at school."

"That will make it all the more adventurous," Severine promised with a glance at the clock. She frowned and then wrapped herself in a black wool coat edged with black fur. She added gloves and sighed. "Time to meet Florette."

"Are you going to tell her about Mr. Oliver?"

"Despite myself," Severine admitted, as she glanced once more in the mirror. She didn't want to admit to the nervousness that made her delay. "I like her."

"I like her too," Lisette said. "She's kind when no one else is. She didn't dive into the trouble with you at the mansion. She didn't side with Andre, and she might like your grandmother, but she doesn't pretend that your grandmother is good to you."

Severine sighed and put money, a handkerchief, a

compact, her lipstick, a small revolver, and her house key into her clutch. She felt only a moment of hesitation about the revolver. She'd requested it from Mr. Brand and he'd delivered and even given her the basic lessons in its use. Where another man might have argued against her carrying it, Mr. Brand had been supportive, even enthusiastic, that she had another form of protection.

She clucked to Anubis. She had insisted upon the dog so often and with such large tips for those who allowed him entry with her, that he'd added to her overall look. That wasn't why she insisted upon him, but the rich, orphan with the massive guard dog was just the level of notoriety that refused her father's old companions from ignoring her. They could disapprove, but they couldn't ignore.

Severine drove the Rolls-Royce Phantom with Anubis in the back seat to retrieve Florette from her parents' house. Florette had moved from Grandmère's home to her parents' home upon their return, and Severine had to go inside to retrieve Florette rather than honk the horn. She did so with a sigh and no trace of eagerness.

"We're not invited?" Barnabé asked with just enough of a pout to plead his case without quite letting go of his manliness.

"I told you we're going shopping," Florette said, and it sounded like she'd said it so often her voice was a little hoarse. "You can romance Severine on another day."

She laughed at the dark look her brother gave her, took Severine's hand, and yanked her out the door. "Come! Mama intends to scold you some more."

Severine didn't delay after that comment. She hurried down the steps and into the auto. Before she'd started the car, the curtains twitched. Aunt Delphine wasn't the type to chase someone out of the doors, so the second they'd gotten beyond the front steps, they'd be safe. That didn't stop Severine from feeling as though they were being chased. They hopped into the car, then she peeled away from the house and Florette giggled as they swung around the corner.

A moment later, Severine slowed the auto down and suggested, "What if we started with a walk?"

"That was said in a way that promises bad news," Florette told Severine. "Have you decided to stop looking into your parents' lives and leave?" Florette sounded sad. "Mama will nag at you until you give in and move in with someone else. I wouldn't stay either. I already am desperate for a reason to escape the house. I can only hope that I can marry soon. It's like they've bound me up in cotton and sheets, and I can't move or breathe. I feel like I've been mummified alive. Grandmère, for all her faults, never really cared if I went shopping with the girls or had luncheon with a beau or even lingered in bed with chocolate and a novel."

"Your mother objects to all of those things?"

"I feel like I need permission to breathe."

Severine laughed and then she stopped near New Orleans Park and got out of the vehicle. Florette followed willingly enough even though she'd told Severine at least a half dozen times that it was incomprehensible that Severine went for such long, lonely walks.

"What is wrong, Severine?" Florette asked. "You have that tight look on your mouth that says you've seen something sour."

"I've learned something sour, and I find that I don't want to tell you."

"Why not?" Florette asked. "What has it to do with me?"

"You're half in love with Mr. Oliver," Severine told her, "and I'm not sure he's a widower."

"What?" Florette asked, her big blue eyes wide and beginning to brim with tears. Severine winced. She opened her clutch and handed over a handkerchief.

"He came here looking for his wife. Mr. Thorne's sister. I don't have any idea where she is, why she was here, or what they expect to find, but he's still in love with her, Florette. Alive, dead, missing, in between, I don't know. But he's gone for her."

Florette spun away from Severine, curling her shoulders into her chest. She was utterly still and quiet for a long, long moment and then she looked up. Severine couldn't see where Florette's eyes were fixed, but after a long while she crossed to a stone bench, took a seat, and arranged her legs prettily.

Any sign of tears was gone. Any sign of distress was gone except that the tightness around the mouth had spread from Severine to Florette.

"I don't think he meant to hurt you," Severine offered, sitting next to her. "He seemed quite upset when I confronted him directly about hurting you."

"Lovely day," Florette said in reply, her fingers clenched hard around the handkerchief. "The way the trees contrast with the sky is simply breathtaking."

Clearly, Florette didn't wish to speak further on the subject. So Severine offered, "The swans in the pond are always nice to see. Shall we wander that way?"

Florette nodded without speaking, and Severine noted

a sudden trembling of her jaw. They walked slowly with Anubis trailing them until they reached the pond. Florette took a seat immediately and Severine gave her several moments to herself by moving closer to the water.

After a while, Florette rose and said with forced brightness, "I should like to have tea."

They walked silently back to the car and as Severine started it again, Florette said softly, "Thank you."

"You're welcome."

Florette sniffed once. "I always did like Bernard Mason."

"I don't believe I know him," Severine said. "But life-long decisions should be made carefully. Especially when carefully manipulating a mother with a comment on the wealth and jewelry Grandmère has to leave behind, and Grandmère taking a deliberate stumble that would mean she would need you as a care companion."

Florette turned slowly towards Severine who parked the auto near the hotel and restaurant.

"What are you saying?"

"I'm saying if you promise to tell Grandmère to give information about me, she'll give you a place to stay and will even ask for you."

Florette stared. "I'm not going to give Grandmère information about you."

"It'll be fine." Severine had no intention of letting Florette truly into her confidence. "Especially if you tell her that you don't feel good about the idea, but that you'll share both ways freely."

"Freely?" Florette's jaw dropped. "But why would either of you benefit from that?"

"Because you're smarter than Grandmère and Andre

believe you to be because you're from my side of the family. Also, she thinks you have a price."

"What if I do?"

"Then I've made a mistake about you. I believe you're principled and kind. I believe that the state of your heart matters to you." Severine's eyes moved over her cousin's face and she added, "You are ready to love, but you deserve the time to find the right man. Your instincts are right, because I believe that Mr. Oliver is exactly the kind of man you'd want to marry. He's twisted up with his missing wife and perhaps, not for you. But just the right kind of man."

"What if nobody like him ever loves me?" Florette sniffed once. "I suppose I liked him rather well."

"Did you love him?"

"How could I?" Florette's jaw tightened. "He side-stepped the things that mattered. He talked about the weather, the people around us. He didn't layer me with compliments and write sonnets about my eyes."

Severine laughed as Florette shot her a sardonic look. "Did you want sonnets?"

"He was kind and attentive. But he didn't really make me believe he loved me. He didn't really lead me on. I led myself on, and now I feel quite stupid."

Severine got out of the auto. "That means we'll have to order two desserts."

"Yes," Florette agreed.

"And perhaps afterwards we'll spend all of our pin money on silk stockings and new dresses."

"Father is home." Florette grinned. "I'm in the mood for a wardrobe beyond my pin money, but happily, I can send the bill to him."

CHAPTER 9

The two-story building was made of brick and had large windows with brick arches over each one, drawing attention to the overall beauty in the details. The second story was surrounded by a wrought-iron balcony that was rife with hanging plants. A woman was hanging over the balcony, smoking a cigarette. Her hair was bobbed and her red dress was fringed, and she seemed to glow with sheer beauty. Perhaps it was the beauty of the area reflecting back to her. Either way, Severine had to pause in sheer admiration.

"It's so different here," she murmured.

"Than the religious wilds of the Austrian mountains?" Lisette asked, raising an eyebrow.

Severine's laugh was low as she checked the buildings for some sign that they'd reached the right place. Anubis huffed as they passed a man playing the saxophone. The wail of the instrument filled the air all around the building and Severine and Lisette paused for a moment to appreciate the soulful call.

"Would the nuns disown you for talking to a medium, fortune teller type?"

"I'm sure they wouldn't be enthusiastic about it, but they don't disown or stop loving. That's not how they're made. They advise with love and kindness."

"My grandmother, my father's mother, would take me by the ear and drown me in holy water for this."

"Didn't your father abandon you? What gives her the right?"

"She stops by here and there to leave judgement. It would have been better," Lisette said without inflection, "if she'd abandoned us too."

Severine reached out and squeezed Lisette's hand and then stepped away to look up at a flowering plant. "It is so beautiful here. Very different from my religious wilds, but yes, so beautiful."

"Which do you prefer?" Lisette asked curiously, her gaze landing on a very tall, very thin fellow at the end of the street. He looked both as if he'd been stretched out and as if he knew her. Severine met his eyes with her own and saw something in them. She wasn't sure what it was, but he had thoughts about Severine. Of that she had little doubt.

"Who is that?" Severine asked.

Lisette's only answer was the shake of a head. She glanced at Severine. "We're here. Are you ready?"

Severine nodded and then followed Lisette around the corner of the building and through a red door in the shadows of the alleyway. It took a long moment for her eyes to adjust to the darkness in the back room. Other than the door, there were no windows in the room. Once she could see, she saw Lisette and one other person in the room.

"This her?" the man asked in a low voice.

"Clearly," Lisette replied dryly.

"Severine DuNoir," Severine said.

"I don't care," he said. "Lisette said you'd pay for what you want to know."

"I will," Severine answered easily, unbothered by the aggressiveness. "But you aren't the fortune teller."

Lisette glanced at Severine, handed the fellow a bill, and then he led the way through the back of the building and out into the courtyard. The flowering lushness wasn't what Severine expected. She also tried to hide her disbelief at the woman waiting for them. The woman had very dark skin, and with the rosiness of her cheeks and the shine of healthfulness, she shone with beauty.

"I expected…"

Severine trailed off and the woman laughed. "Skulls and chickens and a snake about my neck?"

"Maybe," Severine admitted. "Something otherworldly and disturbing."

"Do you have the gift?" Lisette asked the woman. "You go by Madame Cocotte. That's not your real name."

"My real name is no concern of yours," Cocotte said. "Madame Cocotte will suffice."

"You'll sell a fortune," Severine asked.

"I've been known to deliver a requested message."

"And you pass information as well." Lisette added. "For a price."

"A girl's got to eat."

"I can understand that," Severine said, taking a seat on a stone bench and giving Lisette a look until she did the same. Cocotte, however, remained standing, keeping a wrought iron table between them.

"We'd like names," Lisette said. "Of anyone who Severine's father, Lukas DuNoir, paid you to give messages to. Whether theatrically or with a clever little note."

"I can't tell you anything." Cocotte smiled easily, a flash of white teeth and quick glance to the side. Severine followed the woman's gaze and saw someone watching them from the building.

Severine lowered her voice so it couldn't be overheard. "I need a list of names and instances."

Cocotte lifted a brow and leaned back, glancing at Lisette as if asking if Severine were serious. Instead, Lisette named an amount.

"I'll take double that, cher. I'm no dumb dora. If people think I've turned on them, it isn't just lettuce that will dry up."

"We already know it's generous," Lisette replied. "We've heard what you charge."

"But this would be for betraying my customers," the woman said, ignoring the fact that Lukas DuNoir was dead.

Severine rose, leaving a straight hundred-dollar bill on the table in such a way that someone watching wasn't able to see it. "Let me know when you want real money. I'll want real names, real situations, and anything you know that concerns me right now."

"One whale isn't worth all of my smaller fish."

How quickly she went from the doubled price of what Severine offered to that being nothing. Severine wasn't even bothered by the switch.

"That's a call you have to make," Severine replied. "I want something verifiable to start. Maybe you could start with Theodosia Grantley."

She then turned and left the courtyard, shaking her head at her assumptions about what she thought before she came to the building. She didn't want to haggle with an unknown audience, so she left. Was it the right move? She wasn't sure. But, she had seen the avarice in Cocotte's gaze, and Severine knew that money talked, persuaded, and changed things. It was far more than a bit of a power.

She stepped into the alley and found the tall, thin man standing there. He eyed her, and she could see a threat in his gaze, but she had her revolver and Anubis, and the fellow wasn't quite as powerful as he seemed to think.

"Girl," he said and smiled slowly in that sort of crazed, evil way that wanted her to be fearful.

"Hello," she replied, eyeing his hands. Sister Mary Chastity had told her to always watch their hands and their eyes. That's where the signs were.

"Come," he told her.

"Who are you?"

Lisette just stepped into the alley behind Severine and gasped.

"Someone wants to talk to you."

"My home is fairly well-known and easily found," she said, glancing at Lisette, who looked more alarmed than Severine expected. "We answer our door when people knock, so it's not as though I'm impossible to see."

"Come," he ordered with menace.

"She's not going anywhere," Lisette told the man. "Get on out of here."

He straightened and broadened and angled his body to loom over them, and Anubis growled low and deep.

"Your dog doesn't have to survive this, girl."

Severine lifted a brow and took hold of Anubis's collar, handing Lisette her clutch and stepping just in front of Lisette, so the retrieval of the revolver would be hidden. "How do you think this is going to happen?"

His reply was a repeat of that crazed grin. "Your father owes people money. They've decided you will pay."

Lisette stepped to the side, holding the revolver on the man. "Bring proof to Mr. Brand, and he'll see it paid."

The weighty look on the man's face said that whatever was owed, there was no proof. "That's not how this works, little girl. Put that pea shooter away. We both know you aren't going to use it. You told me once you had a horror of guns."

Severine held out her free hand and Lisette gave her the revolver while Anubis growled.

"What you think? I'll fear you instead?" His mean voice made Severine want to let Anubis loose. In a bound or two, her sweet boy would have his jaws around the man's neck.

"Back away," Severine ordered with the background music of Anubis's low, fierce growl. Her dog's growl bothered her far more than the man's threats. Anubis was a reliable judge of a person's intent, and the fierceness of that rumble had Severine's gaze narrowing.

"Make me," he said, ignoring the revolver to laugh at her.

She lifted a brow and shot the ground at his feet.

He cursed and leapt back, and she saw his eyes widen.

"The next one doesn't have to be in the ground."

There were shouts in the street, and she smirked at him. "What do you think? One man, cornering two women in an alley. Will they help you or me?"

His answer was to turn and run. Severine handed Lisette the gun again and took better hold of Anubis, who hadn't relaxed as the fellow disappeared.

"Mr. Brand is never going to let me leave the house again," Severine muttered low and Lisette laughed, but they were both shaky. Severine let out a near hysterical giggle while Lisette wiped a quick tear away.

"Lady, you all right?" a man asked. "Was that you?"

"We're all right," Severine told him with relief, looking at the man who faced the potential crime scene with a readiness to help. "Thank you for coming."

"Did you hear that shot?"

"I heard it," Severine hedged. "I saw someone running."

The fellow nodded and looked back down the street. "Be careful, miss." His gaze landed on Anubis and then said, "Maybe you're all right with that beast following you around."

"I am," Severine replied as though she wasn't feeling a little jittery and headed towards where they had left her car. She wasn't even surprised to see that someone had cut all of the tires. They'd wanted her helpless and afraid. And she shivered as she faced it.

"Miss?" someone called from the restaurant across the street. Severine looked up, and he said, "I can send one of my boys for a mechanic."

"Would you?" Severine asked and closed her eyes. "Might you also have a telephone I can use?"

The man nodded and Severine and Lisette took an outside table after Lisette called Mr. Brand for help. Severine closed her eyes and realized that her hands were shaking. She'd been calm when the man was trying to scare her. She'd been calm when she'd made her way back to the car as though it were safer for her than being on foot, but now that they had help, her hands were shaking.

The restaurant fellow brought them crab and corn chowder along with a basket of bread. They hadn't ordered it, but Severine took a bite and focused on the scent, the temperature, the flavors in her mouth. She counted things she could hear until her hands stopped shaking and then, when she looked up again, her skin didn't feel so foreign.

"Did you see who did it?" Severine asked when the restaurant owner checked on them again.

"One of the boys saw who did it, but the fellow was angled away, so we didn't see his face. My boy chased after him, but he disappeared."

"Was he very tall and very thin?" Lisette asked. "Medium dark skin with a scar on his jawline?"

Severine's gaze narrowed. She hadn't seen the scar, and she couldn't help but remember the recognition when they'd seen the man before they'd visited Cocotte. A flash of distrust moved through Severine. Could she trust Lisette? Could she trust this man, for that matter? Maybe the soup was drugged like the wine at the mansion.

From what she'd been experiencing, Severine felt that the people she'd been around since she'd come to New Orleans were a bit too quick to put something in someone's drink. The doctored wine at those Spirit Society events that made one a bit more likely to be overcome by the 'supernatural.' The wine that had put her right to sleep at the big house when her brother had been trying to make her think she was mad.

Maybe she was being hunted on all sides, and she couldn't trust anyone. But did she want to live like that? She considered how many times that Lisette had comforted and protected her and then sat up straighter.

"This is driving me mad."

"The car?" Lisette asked as the mechanic arrived and Severine rose.

"No, the number of people who are convenient. Was our friend inside a bystander with a good heart? Or was he somehow purchased? What about that fellow? Why do you know he has a scar? I know I can trust you, but the paranoid feeling is rising, and I find myself just wanting to return to Austria where everyone was trustworthy."

"I knew him when I was younger," Lisette told Severine. "I helped take care of him after he got that scar. Mama sewed him up. I nursed him through a fever. I trusted him once."

"But you don't now?"

Lisette's laugh was dark and there was a wealth of pain behind it. "Not in the least."

"What shall I do?"

"We need to be careful, Sev. This isn't over yet."

Severine nodded and then crossed to the mechanic who eyed her car and said, "This is a damn shame, miss. A damn shame."

"Can you fix it?"

"I'll need some time. This fellow says there was something with your gas tank, miss. I think it would be good to drain it, just in case. If the fiend who did this wanted to ruin this beauty, he could have put sugar in your gas tank."

Severine nodded, deeply comforted by the fury on the man's face. She agreed with him on the things to be done and then found Mr. Brand had arrived. He'd stayed in the background while she spoke to the mechanic and then just nodded at the fellow.

"I'll accompany the car to the shop, Severine," Mr. Brand told her, "and then get a ride home. You'll be all right with my car?"

She nodded and then said with a sigh, "We need to speak when you return."

He knew her well enough to see the worry. "Do you want me to come with you now?"

She shook her head, paid the restaurant man, tipped the fellow who'd tried to save her car, and headed back home with Lisette and Anubis, hoping to feel safe in the walls that had always protected her.

CHAPTER 10

"There's a letter for you," Chantae said as they entered.

"Is it urgent?" Severine asked, feeling that haunting chill. She imagined hearing her father enter the house behind her, slamming the door and calling, I'm home, my loves. How had he entered the house when he'd visited his mistresses? Had he ever visited the son who was Severine's age?

Those thoughts were chased away by the energetic greeting of her two girls, Kali and Persephone. Severine knelt down to accept their love and let the huffs of excitement and adoration chase away the ghost of her father.

She looked up her from her position and asked, "Who's it from?"

"That Grantley woman."

Severine considered for a moment and murmured, "I wonder if she realized she's being followed or if it's about her haunting."

Lisette shrugged. "She makes it seem like she's harder

and more experienced than I would have guessed for a spoiled wife. Maybe she did spot the tail."

"Either way," Severine said suddenly, "I'm taking a long, long bath. Don't answer the door for anyone."

"Anyone?" Lisette asked.

"Well," Severine paused to consider who she truly trusted and what she actually wanted. Finally she said, "Florette, Mr. Brand, Mr. Thorne, Mr. Oliver. Anyone else, don't even open the door."

Chantae's gaze widened while Lisette said, "I'll explain, Mama."

"Your granny is here. Should we send her home?" Chantae asked, her gaze moving from Severine to Lisette. There was clear worry in Chantae's face for her own mother.

Severine shook her head and then said, "I think being alone is a bad idea for any of us. Call for a driver and a car if your mother needs to go home and have them take her all the way."

"Meline was going to come by," Lisette said. "I should try to stop her."

"If you can," Severine agreed. "If you can't, make sure you send her home in a car. I'll happily pay to get her all the way to her door safely."

Severine pressed her hand against her forehead and then sighed. She'd been ignoring the tightness in her neck, and the headache had moved from tight to pounding. Her eyes hurt in their sockets, and her spine was stiff from her skull to her hips.

"Are you all right?" Chantae asked.

Severine pushed her face into Persephone's neck and shook her head against the dog's ruff. She quietly said something incomprehensible and then added, "Don't let the dogs out either. Keep one with you in the kitchen and if they become alarmed, you should be too."

Chantae's gaze widened even further, and then narrowed. "We'll be fine."

"Yes, we will," Severine agreed. "They think we're weak."

"They're wrong," Lisette replied.

"We are going to peel back all of those layers, find the man, and stop him. Is the daily girl still here?"

Chantae nodded.

"Would you send her up with a cup of Sister Bernadette's tea blend? And when the maid goes home, call the car for her."

Whatever the reply was, she didn't hear. Severine pressed both hands against her temples and rubbed, hoping to release some of the tension. She rose and found her way to her bedroom with Anubis and Persephone at her heels.

She had taken one of the guest rooms when she'd returned, unable to stomach her parents' bedroom. The comment about redoing the house and making it her own echoed in her head, and rather than going straight to her bedroom, she dared to open her parents' door instead.

The scent of her mother's perfume still lingered, or perhaps, Severine was just going mad. She took a deep breath and a step into the room. Anubis growled and she followed his gaze to her mother's dressing table. The three mirrors and vanity were covered, but Severine would swear that she sensed her mother sitting there, brushing her hair.

When Severine had lingered in the room as a child, Mother would snap at her. *What do you want, Severine?*

Don't sneak about like a goblin. It makes you quite unde-sirable.

Severine shuddered and shut the door on her mother's presence. She turned and crossed to her bedroom. She must have spent longer in her mother's bedroom than she'd realized as there was a teapot and teacup on a platter with berries, cookies, cheese, and crackers. Severine poured herself a cup of tea and then took two aspirin. She sighed as she slumped onto the end of her bed and then sipped the tea. She could so easily envision the nuns with this tea in her hands, the scent in the air. Harsh, aching desire to see the nuns again filled Severine to the point where she hurt from her hair to her toes.

The letter from Mrs. Grantley was staring at her from her dresser, but Severine ignored it, finished the tea, and then leaned back to let the aspirin begin to work. When she was able to drag herself back up, she filled the bath with salts and oils and then slid into the water.

SEVERINE FOUND HER WAY DOWNSTAIRS, unashamedly wearing black silk pajamas and a red and black kimono. Her hair was hidden under a black silk turban, and her skin was free of cosmetics. It wasn't even dinnertime yet, but she was done for the day. She wanted to curl up with a novel and breathe easily.

She discovered Chantae and the daily maid in the kitchen. Their maids changed often since Chantae was precise and demanding, and they were still looking for the right fit. Severine smiled and then laughed at the look on Chantae's face.

"I'm hungry," Severine whined like a child and then laughed again as Chantae gazed at her up and down.

"You back to your baby days? You want I should get you a nurse? I don't hold with whining from grown women."

Severine shook her head. "Anubis and Persephone need to visit the garden, and I have no desire to do anything else today. I was giving serious thought to diving under my covers and not coming out, but I'm also having serious thoughts about something to drink."

Chantae snorted and then crossed to the cupboard and mixed Severine a cocktail with fresh juice, lime, and gin. Severine grinned at both Chantae and the daily maid, who seemed surprised at the alcohol. Technically, it wasn't illegal to drink alcohol—just to manufacture or buy it. And she'd done neither. Mr. Brand had stocked the house for Severine, and she hadn't asked questions.

Instead, Severine took her drink and then found Lisette in the library. She looked up from her seat near the fire and then lifted the book so Severine could read the title. It was another Brontë book, and Severine crossed to the shelf and took down a copy of Jane Eyre. She curled up across from Lisette, who asked, "What was in the letter? Do you feel better?"

"Yes, I feel better, and no, I refused to read it yet."

Lisette lifted a brow. Severine laughed and winced at the same time. "I will." There was a fat edge of a whine in her voice, and she winced at that too.

She settled back in the comfortable chair, opened her book, and then sighed when she heard the doorbell. Lisette rose to answer the door, commanding Kali to heel. Severine couldn't help but note the heavy weight in the cardigan that Lisette had put on over her day dress to hide the pistol. So, it had come to being armed when they answered the door. Were Lisette's worries based upon Severine's actions or her own knowledge of the man with the scar?

Severine followed, sticking her head out of the library door to watch as Lisette peeked through the hole and then started to unlatch the door. It wasn't until that moment that Severine realized exactly how many locks they had on the door. There were a good half-dozen bolts and chains.

She could remember them from her childhood, and she could envision her father locking them when he came home from the office. Her gaze narrowed as she realized what so many locks meant.

Her father had felt the need for them. Clearly, she thought, he hadn't been wrong. Was that why he'd purchased the big mansion in the country? Was it more than having a showpiece? A castle that announced exactly how rich Lukas DuNoir was and how well he'd won the race?

Lisette glanced back at a sound Severine must have made and said, "It's Mr. Brand."

She considered changing and then refused. She was home and didn't want to change. If he were her guardian and brother, he could stand to see her with her hair up, her face free of cosmetics, and her swathed in layers of silk in the form of pajamas and a kimono rather than a chemise and a dress.

Mr. Brand looked between the women. His surprise at all the locks being in place during the day completely bypassed whatever shock he might have felt to find Severine so comfortably attired.

"What is going on?" he asked.

Severine saw him take note of the dog at Lisette's feet, pause on the shape underneath her sweater, and then he turned from her to Severine.

"We were threatened today," Lisette told him.

"Plus the damage to the car," Severine added.

"Did they say what they wanted?" Mr. Brand stepped into the house and then glanced back. "Mr. Oliver and Mr. Thorne have just arrived home. Shall I wave them over?"

"I think we had better," Severine said. "We don't know which of our inquiries caused whoever needed to threaten us to lash out after the last few months of nothing other than Andre's lurking."

Mr. Brand nodded and turned, calling, "Gents. Time for a conference?"

When the men crossed the street and came to the door, Severine lifted her cocktail. Mr. Oliver's jaw dropped at the sight of her in pajamas, but Severine announced, "Drinks for everyone. I'm sorry I don't have enough kimonos for all of us, but if you want to dive into the kimono club, Lisette, Meline sent a few for me to look over."

Lisette snorted. "I'll stick with the drinks over the kimonos, but perhaps, I'll have two cocktails, cher."

"Two for everyone," Severine announced. Mr. Thorne's eyes moved over her, and he asked, "Are you all right?"

"She's not," Lisette answered before Severine could shuffle off the worry. "Neither of us are, really. We found Madame Cocotte. When we left, there was a man."

"A man?" Mr. Brand demanded, his eyes moving between the two of them, and then he took them each by the arm, and pulled them—gently—into the parlor and seated them near the fire. He glanced at Thorne and said, "Drinks, please."

Mr. Brand pulled a chair over, fixing his gaze on them equally. "Tell me everything."

"His name is Landon Gentry," Lisette said. "I've known him since I was five, and he was eleven, and he was my first love."

Mr. Brand leaned back in surprise and his gaze moved to Severine. She felt the weight of it, but she didn't look at him. She was too busy examining her friend. Lisette's eyes shone with unshed tears, and even though Lisette had once told Severine that she wasn't in love with anyone, Severine suddenly realized that Lisette had been in love once. Desperately in love. In love enough that the pain still remained even after the love had gone.

While Lisette struggled for control, Mr. Thorne handed her a drink and then passed another to Mr. Brand. Mr. Oliver was already pouring himself one while the rest of them turned their attention back to Lisette.

"He got involved with someone," she finally continued. "Someone powerful. He never said who. But the way he walked changed, the way he talked, the way he treated people. We went from being neighbors to bugs. Even me. Even though he had cared about me before. Maybe even loved me. But"—Lisette shook her head—"that part doesn't matter anymore. He changed. The last time I saw him, he had been hurt. Someone had nearly, but not quite cut his neck. He couldn't go to the hospital. Mama and I took care of him. Nursed him back to health. When we asked questions—"

Lisette shook her head again, but whatever memory she was experiencing had her hands shaking. Severine put her own drink down to reach out and steady Lisette.

"I don't know who he works for," Lisette said, low. The words were directed to Severine. Those wide brown eyes were shiny with tears and the mascara on her thick, beautiful lashes would smudge soon. Severine might even join in with sympathy tears if things carried on.

"All right then," Severine said. "I believe you."

"But—"

Severine shot Mr. Oliver such a dark look, that he held up his hands in surrender.

"I really don't know," Lisette told Severine again.

"We have a place to start now, don't we? A man to follow? A face to watch for. We're ahead."

"He's not a good man, Sev," Lisette told her. "He's not. It doesn't matter that I loved him once, you can't trust him. Not with any part of you."

"I won't," Severine replied softly. "We won't."

"What do we need to do?" Mr. Brand asked.

Lisette's face was earnest and worried when she said, "Arm yourself. Don't go anywhere alone. Keep an eye on your cat and our dogs."

"We'll hire guards," Mr. Brand said. "Severine, I want to bring someone in from outside of here. I know some men from my army days that are honorable and reliable. They'll look after you."

Severine paused, and the fear on Lisette's face was convincing.

"No more rotating daily maids," Mr. Brand added. "Take the one you know the best and who can't be bought. Someone you can trust and deal with whatever she doesn't do perfectly."

This time, Lisette nodded. "I'll take care of it. I know who." She paused and then asked, "Can Granny stay here?"

"Of course," Severine told Lisette. "Of course, of course."

She leaned back and then glanced at the others.

"This man confronted you?" Mr. Thorne asked, and Severine saw the flexing muscle of his jaw.

"He wanted us to go with him."

"How did you get away?" Mr. Oliver demanded. "Surely he was able to overpower you? Neither of you are all that…powerful."

"The dog," Severine said.

Lisette snorted. "Severine shot the ground at his feet. He ran when people came running to help."

Mr. Thorne's jaw dropped. "You were carrying a weapon?"

"You can use a weapon?" Mr. Oliver demanded.

"You felt the need to use it?" Mr. Brand finished. He cursed low and didn't bother to apologize as usual. Instead he cursed again and rose to pace.

Severine, however, leaned back and sipped her drink.

"Then your car." Mr. Brand cursed again. "You need to take a chauffeur. We'll have one of the guards drive it. He'll be armed. I don't want to spirit you away like a princess in a tower, but I can suddenly see the point of those fathers who did."

"Dragons aren't safer for the princess," Lisette told him dryly. "And a tower alone sounds like a safe road to madness."

Severine crossed her fingers over her chest. "Is it because Mrs. Grantley is working with us? Perhaps someone realized she was?"

Mr. Brand turned and then demanded, "How could they know?"

"How do they know anything?" Lisette muttered. "Has anything else changed?"

Mr. Brand muttered and said, "Since Severine has been home, I've stopped maintaining business as usual. Those were my previous instructions. Severine wanted to know what she owned and what the investments were supporting. I've been tracking those down."

"You've been asking questions," Mr. Thorne repeated, emphasis on the questions. The weight behind the emphasis was enough to convey that questions were dangerous without him needing to say so.

"Someone is spooked," Osiris Oliver said for all of them, stating the obvious.

"Perhaps the status quo is safer," Mr. Brand sighed. He shook his head, and Severine didn't need to tell him that the status quo would never be enough for her.

"My father was a criminal." Severine's announcement was unnecessary, but she needed to say it for herself. "I won't be."

CHAPTER 11

The letter from Mrs. Grantley was a demand for action. It contained the location of a key at the Grantley mansion and an even more stringent order for a presence in the house that very evening.

I haven't slept for days, Mrs. Grantley had written. The haunting has been taken to another level as though whoever is behind this madness has changed tactics entirely. Before the last party, there was some activity near the witching hour which faded within the hour.

"It's not good," Mr. Thorne said, "that tactics have changed. The more casual haunting could have been an idiotic grandchild having a hoax on Grandmama. Leaving an old woman sleepless day after day would speed an already dying woman to the grave."

Severine bit at her bottom lip for a moment. "Before I decided to return home, I was sleepless for days. It turned me into a bumbling idiot."

"Are you saying that someone is doing that to Mrs. Grantley purposefully?" Lisette breathed in shock. Her eyes moved from person to person and then she mumbled about the privileged rich.

Mr. Brand rose and paced before the fire as Severine answered, "I just couldn't help but remember how it felt."

"It's possible that someone is wanting to make her look incompetent," Mr. Brand said, facing them from near the fire and then letting his hand rest on Anubis. He sighed. "The Grantleys, along with several others, are part of a business investment scheme. Your father was part of it, and you still are."

"So?" Severine demanded.

"So," Mr. Brand replied. "Her children are part of it too. If someone were wanting her vote to be curtailed, that might be a reason to drive her into seeming incapable."

"Or it could be her evil grandchildren," Lisette said, seeming to like that idea. "It's good to know that the super-rich aren't any happier than those of us who worry for our pennies."

"Sister Sophie used to say happiness is directly related to the state of our souls, I think," Severine replied. "Gratitude and the like more than anything else."

"Sister Sophie is my favorite," Mr. Brand told Severine.

"I like Sister Bernadette," Lisette announced.

"I met that one," Mr. Brand told Lisette with a bit of a twinkle in his eye and a grin on his face. "She was cantankerous."

Severine chuckled. Sister Bernadette appealed to Lisette because the nun redefined ornery. Well that, and because Sister Bernadette liked to play in the garden with anything that was dangerous. Severine rubbed her chest at the ache of missing her nuns. If only they weren't so very far away.

Mr. Thorne had reread the letter and he said, "She's demanding both of us, Miss DuNoir."

The return to formal names continued to be painful.

"I don't like the idea of you going," Mr. Brand told her, "especially after this afternoon. Even with Mr. Thorne, it's just—we don't know why that man wanted to bring you somewhere or to whom he was supposed to bring you."

"You can't trust anything he said. Not even that he was supposed to bring her somewhere else."

"It'll be all right," Severine told them. "Mr. Thorne and Anubis will be present. I'll have my little peashooter."

"We'll drop you nearby," Mr. Brand told Severine. "Whoever is doing this would be suspicious to see an extra vehicle. I can wait in the car in case you need us. I've got a whistle that we can use as a signal. You blow it three times, and I'll come running."

"I've got a peashooter myself, cher." Lisette smiled. "We won't let the lads step out without backup of the lady sort. Us girls are a little more aggressive, I think."

Mr. Brand chuckled, not realizing that Lisette was serious. She winked and said, "We'll take a separate car in case one of us needs to go for help. Shall we change our clothes?" Lisette's expression said Severine needed to change from her pajamas.

Severine winked in reply.

SEVERINE LEFT them and decided on a simple black dress, a black cardigan, black stockings and sturdy shoes. She had no idea what lay ahead, but figuring out what was happening to Mrs. Grantley would move Severine a step forward on peeling back another layer of her father's life.

She examined herself in the mirror before she left her room. She'd left the turban on, so she looked a bit like an acolyte. Simple black clothes, something black on her head. She paused and then reached through her jewelry box, adding the beautiful silver cross that Sister Mary Chastity had given her when she'd left the nunnery.

Perhaps an emblem of love from the nuns was just what Severine needed to see her through this day. She made her way back down the stairs with a bag over her shoulder. It was the sort of thing a student might carry, and she'd added Jane Eyre, her loaded revolver, a lead for Anubis, and a notebook with a few pencils. She added extra money as a general precaution along with her house keys.

Severine found Mr. Thorne waiting for her in the parlor. Mr. Brand was pacing again, and both his mouth and eyes were tight with worry.

"Don't look like that," she told him. "I'll have Anubis and Mr. Thorne, and you and Lisette can have tomorrow night while the rest of us wait in the auto instead, and we'll be quite uncomfortable like you are tonight. Mr. Oliver?" Severine turned to the man and asked, "Will you keep an eye on our house?"

He nodded. "I'll just wait here until you return. Brand and Lisette should take one of the dogs, we'll keep the other."

"We're taking my love, Kali," Lisette announced. "Mama has a preference for Persephone, and Persephone is protective of Mama."

"Persephone is my angel," Chantae said, handing over a basket and two thermoses. "What's all this? Is Lisette going now? I will make more food. You can't trust anything from Mrs. Grantley's kitchens. You might not need the food, but the coffee will see you through the night."

Mr. Thorne took the basket, but Chantae only handed him one of the thermoses. Severine watched his mouth tighten as he realized that Chantae didn't fully trust him with something that Severine might partake of and Mr. Thorne didn't like it in the least.

Severine opened the thermos and sniffed. "That does smell good. Café au lait?"

"Certainly, cher," Chantae replied. "What else?"

Severine leaned in and kissed Chantae on the cheek and added, "Keep an eye on sweet Persephone."

"I will, cher," Chantae added. "You be safe, little one."

Severine turned to Mr. Brand, whose brow was still wrinkled. "I promised your father I'd look after you. I feel like I'm failing."

"I thought you promised him that you'd let me make my own way." Severine crossed to him and squeezed his hand. "He wanted me to bury myself in my own way."

"I did promise that," Mr. Brand groaned. "I hate myself for it. I should have promised I'd keep you safe instead. I thought it was understood at the time, but I bet you were the same then as you are now. Only smaller. He knew what he was doing, and I was a chump."

Severine laughed and told him, "I found courage and conviction after my father died. He had little idea about me."

"The seeds of who you'd become were there, Severine. He talked about you often. Say what you will about Lukas DuNoir, he was a good judge of character. I imagine he reflected on yours rather than most."

Severine shook her head, disbelieving. "Shall we go, Mr. Thorne?"

He nodded.

Lisette just came into the room before they left. She paused, glanced between them and then said, "It'll be all right."

Lisette's eyes shifted to Mr. Thorne without him seeing the movement of her eyes.

Severine nodded only the slightest amount to agree. She didn't like that Thorne and Oliver hadn't been open with Severine and her friends. On the other hand, a missing sister was a powerful motive.

Within minutes, Severine let Mr. Thorne lead the way to the car. His black car was entirely unremarkable. Just behind it was Mr. Brand's flashier car where Kali was being let into the back seat. She and Mr. Thorne let Anubis into the back of Mr. Thorne's car. Then he opened the passenger seat for Severine.

As he got into the driver's seat, Severine said, "I bet you could drive this car anywhere and be rather sneaky with it."

He looked at her out of the corner of his eye as he started the car. "That might have been my purpose with its purchase."

Awkward silence filled the auto. Then she took a deep breath and stated, "Lovely weather today."

Mr. Thorne sighed darkly. "I would tell you if I could. I would tell you the whole story with all the gritty details that will haunt me to my grave. It's not my story to tell though. Not mine alone."

Severine nodded.

"I don't want this to ruin our alliance."

She had to admit it hurt her to hear it called an alliance. She would have preferred friendship. There was a tiny voice in her head that was wishing for something else, too. A voice that was demanding her to acknowledge that she'd been partially in love or willing to be in love and now that part of her was being smothered.

Severine asked, "Can you tell me anything about your sister?"

"Her name was Jane. Such a plain little name. Plain Jane." He sounded so sad that Severine felt it in her heart.

"But Jane wasn't plain?"

Mr. Thorne cleared his throat, and it took him a long time to answer. If it weren't dark outside, would she have seen emotion in his eyes? Were they shining? Was his loss evident or was he feeling something else?

"She was perfect."

The car fell to silence, only this time it wasn't so awkward. When they arrived at the Grantley mansion outside the city the tone between them had shifted back to something else.

CHAPTER 12

"What are they thinking?" Severine muttered as Grayson Thorne leaned down and found the brick near the side door. It had clearly been hidden there for some time.

Grayson lifted the key from the indention in the dirt. "I wonder if this is how they're getting in."

"I wonder if this means that whoever is trying to haunt Mrs. Grantley knows her well enough to know about this key?"

Severine examined the house and considered. How hard was it to get inside? Were the servants careful about the locks on the windows and the doors? Was there a door with a malfunctioning entrance that was a sort of open secret? How long would it take her to sidle her way into the house if she wanted to do so? Even without the key? Severine guessed it wouldn't be that difficult.

Perhaps someone Mrs. Grantley trusted was behind this scheme. The letter had said the activities always

104

started after midnight. Severine and Grayson unlocked the side door, keeping the key rather than returning it.

Severine hissed, "Look at this lock."

She turned the flashlight onto the keyhole and it was covered in scratches.

"Lock picks?" she whispered.

"Possibly," he breathed back.

When had those scratches been made? Some of them looked rather new.

They crept into the house as though they hadn't been invited. Mrs. Grantley only had one servant who stayed in the house overnight. There was a carriage house where the butler and housekeeper/cook, a married couple, lived.

Beyond those two was a woman who acted as a generalized helper and who was there to see to Mrs. Grantley should she need anything in the middle of the night. Mrs. Grantley said the old servant slept like the dead. It had been the complaint of her grandchildren, and Severine had to wonder—now that she was in the house—how those grandchildren even knew that the woman slept so hard.

Mrs. Grantley kept no other servants, only hiring when she needed one or two for dinner parties and gatherings and bringing them in from the city.

Severine grabbed Grayson's arm a moment later when she heard a creak on the stairs. They were in a side hallway that led only to that side entrance for servants to use. According to Mrs. Grantley, no one should be on the stairs.

Was it just an old house settling? Anubis was on alert, and Severine couldn't quite decide if that was because she was alarmed or if because he knew exactly what was on the stairs.

"There was no sign of a vehicle," Grayson said so low it was almost just a breath.

"There are other place to leave an automobile," Severine whispered back. "Or a fellow could walk or be dropped off."

There was another sound and Severine said, "There have to be servants' stairs in this big old place."

"Probably near the kitchens," Grayson agreed. He led the way with the attitude of a man who was prepared to throw himself in front of her. Did he know that it had looked as though her father had done just that for her mother? How many nights had she slept in the nunnery, curled into her blankets, wondering if her father had tried to save her mother or if the way they fell was just happenstance.

They found the servants' stairs in a doorway just before the kitchen. The door looked like it hid a closet, and a thin, sharp stairway on the other side led to the second floor.

"Did you hear that?" Grayson asked, suddenly pausing.

Severine's eyes widened and Anubis whined low. She whispered a command, "Anubis, ruhig."

After a long moment of silence, there was nothing. A moment later, she heard a low scratching sound, and she shivered. Her dog's ears tilted forward, and he let out a low rumble, trying to be quiet as she'd commanded.

"It's probably only branches on the window," Grayson said.

Severine rolled her eyes and they waited again until long, long moments passed. The house fell back to a weighty silence.

"Damn it," Grayson muttered, "none of this feels right."

"Maybe this is all meant for us," Severine suggested in a low whisper.

"You think she's part of trapping us?"

"After Andre, trust is difficult even with those who have earned it. Mrs. Grantley has not."

If Mrs. Grantley wasn't setting them up, she was the victim here. And, if Mrs. Grantley were a different woman, this haunting would seem cruel indeed.

For Lisette's mother or grandmother who had a respect for the spirits and a true belief, the idea of them disrupting either of the women's lives would have disrupted their peace in every aspect. For Mrs. Grantley, however, there was an edge of hope to the haunting. What if it was her dead husband? Someone who was truly, utterly cruel would provide that edge of hope and snatch it away.

"I don't know," Severine said. "If I were her enemy, I might think a vengeful haunting is just the thing to ruin her passing. She's so firm about dying. I think there must be a reason for that certainty."

They had reached the landing just outside the second floor. The way was lit only by their flashlights, and the light seemed to be losing the battle against the dark. The shadows were thick and deep below and above.

She shivered, too easily able to imagine a fiend from the other world at the base of the stairs. She licked her lips and then froze, once again, when she heard a creaking sound. It was clearer now and far more than a branch against the window.

Grayson heard it as well, and he shuddered ahead of her. "It's the not knowing that's the worst," he told her low.

"What do you mean?"

"I mean is it a criminal terrorizing an old woman or a friend trying to satisfy Mrs. Grantley's desire to connect with the other side? Is it something else? Something—I don't know."

"Something supernatural?"

"I don't think it is," Grayson muttered as a high-pitched cackle filled the air. It seemed to come from all sides, and it was far, far louder than it should have been.

Severine gasped and Anubis growled.

"What the devil?" Grayson demanded.

"What the human?" Severine murmured even though her hand was pressed over her chest and her heart was racing.

"Turn off the flashlight," Grayson told her. "We'll draw too much attention if they're just there."

He slowly opened the door and they realized the hallway was entirely dark. Had the electricity gone out? Severine reached out, searching for a light switch and found it. She flipped it.

Nothing.

She tried again.

Nothing.

She took a deep breath, and placed her hand on Grayson's. He whispered, "I've got one hand on the wall, stay just behind me."

Severine let him keep her hand, tucked the flashlight in her bag, and put her other hand on Anubis's collar.

The cold, high-pitched laugh happened again, and Severine clenched her mouth closed to prevent a reaction beyond leaping out of her skin. On the other side of the door to the servants' staircase, the sound was more other-worldly. Should they chase the sound or pursue the reason behind the lights being out?

She felt her heart in her throat, and her skin was crawling with goosebumps. It was only then that she realized how very cold it was in the hallway.

Grayson took a small step forward, and Anubis huffed once. Severine could feel the tension in the dog's body. He was a good judge of character, she reminded herself, and he didn't like whatever was happening.

What was he sensing? How she wished he could speak. He huffed, and she was sure he was telling her something. She considered reaching for her gun, but she didn't want to accidentally hurt someone in the dark.

Slowly, Severine let go of Grayson to reach out on her own.

"What are you doing?" he whispered.

Rather than holding Anubis back, she let him lead the way. He stepped forward, and she could tell from the pressure of him against her body that he was in a protective mode. He pressed just in front of her, and his form vibrated.

The wail from earlier started again, and he growled low in his throat. It was barely audible, but there was a low gasp. Severine quickly tugged Anubis to the side, moving instinctively away from where she'd been a moment before, and she heard a thump.

Anubis pulled from her grasp, and a very human scream followed. Severine gasped and flipped on her flashlight. The form was a man, dressed all in black, with something over his face that made him entirely unidentifiable, and Anubis had his jaw clenched on a wrist. Severine screamed a moment later when the man swung something towards her dog.

"Here now!" Grayson shouted.

Severine swung her bag, throwing off the aim of the

man, as he struck out at Anubis with thick, heavy object. He pulled his leg back to kick Anubis, but before the man's foot could land on her dog, Grayson dove at the man.

Severine gasped, flailing about on the wall for a light switch, for anything that would prevent this from being two men and her dog fighting in the dark. She felt a light switch and tried it. It was as useless as the first.

The sound of fists landing, grunts, and growls had Severine panicking. What to do? What to do? She finally aimed the flashlight at the struggling men and found that Anubis hadn't let go of the man's wrist. The man, however, had dropped the truncheon. Severine kicked it away from the struggling men and squatted to pick it up.

She looked for a chance to strike the fellow, but as she watched, he kicked out hard, sending Grayson grunting out of reach. The man twisted and rose, aiming a fist at Anubis, and she shouted, "Anubis, hier." Anubis dropped his hold on the man's wrist. The man fled clutching his wrist, and Grayson pushed himself to his feet to dart after him.

"Grayson!" she called.

He looked back, and she tossed him the truncheon.

"Stay here," he ordered.

Severine would have rolled her eyes at him, but he was already gone. Instead, she found her way down the hallway until she found a set of double doors. She opened the door and turned the flashlight onto the bed. In the middle of the bed, Theodosia Grantley was huddled with her knees pulled to her chest.

Severine started to speak and then paused when she heard tapping on the window. "Is there a tree outside of there?"

Slowly, Mrs. Grantley shook her head. Her eyes were wide and horrified.

"Is it always like this?"

Mrs. Grantley shook her head again. She wasn't crying, but she also wasn't making a noise. She was so silent, Severine wondered if the woman was frozen silent in fear.

"There was a man," Severine told her. "Mr. Thorne is chasing him down. What can you tell me?"

"Was it my husband? His portrait is just there."

Severine turned her head and flashlight to look at the man, but she was shaking her head before her eyes ever landed on it. "He had something on his face. Would you have expected your husband to have struck out at me with a truncheon without notice?"

The too long pause made Severine wonder just who Mrs. Grantley and her husband were, and what Severine had been pulled into. That thought was immediately followed by the recognition that her own father was the reason these Grantleys were in her life, both dead and alive. Who was her father? What had he been doing? And just where would this pursuit to understand what had happened to him land her and her friends?

CHAPTER 13

Severine checked the lamp in Mrs. Grantley's room and found it turned on without a problem. She scowled and then returned to the dark hallway, telling Mrs. Grantley, "Stay here."

She snorted at herself when she realized she ordered the woman the same way that Grayson Thorne had ordered her. Had he caught the man? Mr. Brand and Lisette were watching the house. Would they be able to help him? She hoped.

An idea occurred to her, and she realized that someone had been making that loud laughing sound from near what was likely the servant's room. Severine guessed that whoever was making that noise was gone, but she had to wonder if it were the servant or if there were someone else. If so, no one could have slept through that, could they?

Severine rubbed the back of her neck and then slowly tried the hallway light again, using the light of Mrs.

Grantley's bedroom and her flashlight. Nothing. Could it be a blown fuse? Or, she frowned deeply, and turned her gaze to the overhead lights and the lamp on a table. Perhaps the problem was much, much simpler than that. Severine pointed her torch at the lamp and reached out for the bulb, testing it.

She shook her head as she turned the bulb back into its place. As light poured from the lamp into the hallway, joining the light from Mrs. Grantley's room, Severine felt her worry de-escalate immediately.

She called Anubis and approached the servants' stair, making her way up where the sound of otherworldly laughter had appeared. Her hand was on Anubis's collar, and she said to him calmly, "If there's a ghost, I think we're both in trouble."

She didn't, however, think it was a ghost. Especially a moment later when Severine heard someone scurrying around upstairs. If not a ghost, perhaps another man capable of overpowering her? Perhaps someone who could throw her down the stairs?

"That," she told her dog, "doesn't sound much like a ghost."

She considered charging down the front stairs where Grayson had gone now that she had verified Mrs. Grantley was at least living, if not well. However, she thought that might actually be the coward's course. She took a deep breath and slowly made her way up the back stairs towards where the noise had come from.

"Anubis, we're a team, right?" Severine said low, trying to make herself feel better.

He sniffed at her hand and then she heard that scurrying noise again. It sounded almost as if there were something in the walls, and even though she'd felt the very real body of the man earlier, she had her hand pressed over her heart to soothe herself. She wasn't new to secret passages in walls.

The stairs were dark, and she'd decided to err on the side of not using the flashlight. Instead, she felt her way up each step, hand pressing against the wall. She reached the top when she went to find her way to the next step and stumbled forward. As she landed, the thud of her knee on the landing caused the scurrying noise to stop.

Severine froze, and she guessed the person behind that noise had done the same. Utter silence pressed down on her, somehow much more difficult to handle than the inexplicable noises. Anubis pressed his nose into her cheek, and she wrapped her arm around his neck by feel, carefully pushing herself up. She crawled forward, accompanied only by the clicking noise of Anubis's claws against the floor.

She bit her lip and cautiously opened the door to that floor while crouched on her hands and knees. Severine pressed her ear to the ground, hoping to hear whoever was there better. A misstep announced the presence of someone that sounded about ten feet away.

Severine gasped and crawled forward, trying to move silently. A low growl filled the air, and Severine closed her eyes in frustration. The growl went from a warning to a furious, deep throttling sound. Severine trusted Anubis enough to throw herself to the side and he pressed against her as though to protect her with his own body. She felt the rush of someone moving past, and the door opened and slammed after them. Whoever it was had moved past sneaking around, and Severine heard the loud clatter of the person nearly throwing himself down the stairs.

Severine had no idea what Anubis had saved her from, but she had little doubt that he had. She pressed her back against the wall and told him, "You really are my favorite creature."

He pressed his nose against her cheek as if trying to understand why she was sitting on the floor in the dark hallway. She rubbed his chest in gratitude, and to see if he was still alarmed. He leaned into her affection and she felt there wasn't a tense muscle in his body, so she slowly pushed herself to her feet.

She hadn't lost her grip on the flashlight so she turned it on and noticed that this portion of the house was little more than a narrow, dark hallway with small and mismatched doors as though leftovers had been used. Severine moved the flashlight, looking for a light switch, and found it a moment later.

The fiends hadn't loosened the lightbulbs up here, but the pitiful light only showcased how little care had been put into this part of the house. One of the bare bulbs had been smashed and the glass was scattered across the floor. Severine's gaze narrowed and she said, "Anubis, bleibe."

Severine threw open the first door and found a metal bed frame on its side, a dresser with the drawers open, and no sign of inhabitation. She shut that door and opened another one. This room wasn't quite so disassembled, but there was nothing to indicate it was being used.

She paused at the next doorway. There was a noise inside the room, and Severine nearly fled. She wasn't ready to face off again, and her growing worry for Grayson Thorne was pressing in her mind, but she decided to pause longer and listen more carefully.

She turned the flashlight back onto Anubis and his tail flopped against the floor. She repeated, "Bleibe, darling."

Then Severine opened the door to the room and found a woman sleeping heavily on a small metal bed. Her arm was flung out and her mouth was open. With each breath, she hauled air in as though it were going to be her last. The rattling noise was nothing other than a horrendous snore.

"Ma'am?" Severine called.

There wasn't even a small reaction. The woman hauled in a big deep breath, and Severine swore that the next breath was even more raging than the first, as though in the face of audience, the woman took it up another notch.

Her breath rattled that time and she snuffled painfully.

"Ma'am?" Severine asked, approaching with careful steps. "Ma'am?"

Severine shone the flashlight on the woman in front of her and noticed a glass next to the bed. She took hold of the woman's shoulder and shook her hard. The woman snuffled and snorted more, but she didn't wake.

Severine crossed to the light and turned it on and found that, again, whoever was behind this mess hadn't bothered with the servant's light. The more Severine thought about it, the more she could imagine whoever had rushed past her had heard her on the stairs. In the moments before Severine had pushed opened the door, had that person reached up and broken the light?

If so, there might be more to see. Severine examined her surroundings, which amounted to only making a small circle in the small room. Two serving dresses and aprons hung on hooks on the wall along with two dresses for off days. A small dresser held underthings and stockings, while a shallow bowl on top of the dresser held a solitary cross on a chain and a simple ring.

The woman had two pairs of shoes and one pair of slippers lined neatly against the wall and a simple coat on a hook behind the door. A Bible was situated on the table next to where she slept, along with a small pitcher of water, a water glass, and a bottle of syrup.

Severine examined the bottle and wondered just what she was seeing and if this...whatever it was...was the reason for the woman to be sleeping so heavily. Severine opened the jar and sniffed deeply before gasping and jerking it away from her nose. Whatever it was, it was powerful, and it seemed to be based off of alcohol and molasses. Severine wouldn't be surprised if this were the type of thing you bought in a dark alley from a snake oil salesman.

She tried another sniff, coughed, and set it back on the table. She left the woman sleeping and made her way back to Anubis. She told him to stay again and checked the next room, finding a red bullhorn, a tin pan, a wooden hammer, several nails, a length of chain, and an easy chair. Severine scowled and then noticed the small table on the other side of the cushioned chair and found three mugs, one with marks of red lipstick, and two others.

Two others! They were all still warm. Severine spun and rushed to the door at the end of the hall, her flashlight in her hand. This time, she put her gun in her hand. She made a quick search of the rest of the floor, aiming the gun when she opened each door, and found nothing more.

She raced down the steps, past Mrs. Grantley's room, ignoring the woman's call as she made another quick search, then out the front of the house where the door had been left wide open. Severine found Grayson sitting on the steps with his handkerchief to his mouth and the truncheon at his side.

Severine cleared her throat at the same time Anubis reached him, and the dog stuck his nose into Grayson's ear. Grayson reached up and took hold of Anubis as reflexively as Severine would have. She slowly made her way down the stairs, and said, "Are you all right?"

CHAPTER 14

"I'll be fine," he replied. "Is Mrs. Grantley all right?"

"Terrified and alone. Probably cursing me for leaving her." Severine took a seat next to him and glanced his way. "The fellow got away?"

"There was another one. I decided not to follow. I believe, however, Mr. Brand did."

Severine nodded. "A woman was involved. I found coffee cups. One had lipstick. I think I ran into the woman since she fled rather than face off with me."

"The servant perhaps?"

Severine shook her head. "The servant has been drugged."

Grayson cursed low and then asked angrily, "What is it with New Orleans and slipping something into someone's drink? It's ridiculous. How many times have you been drugged? At least twice? Oliver and I have both experienced it. Brand?"

Severine shook her head. She had no idea if Mr. Brand had been drugged before as well. It was as if whoever had started the madness with the little something in someone else's drink had made it acceptable for anyone to do the same.

Severine watched as Grayson dabbed at his lip. She was surprised by a desire to take the handkerchief from him and care for him herself. Instead, she rose from the step and said, "I'll tell Mrs. Grantley that her servant is drugged and see if she wants to go…I don't know…find a hotel."

"She can't stay with you?" Grayson's mischievous smile tugged right at Severine's heart, and she told herself it was the excitement. She added that things between them were not anything other than allies working to separate ends with separate purposes.

"Despite being heavily influenced by nuns for the last half-dozen years, I find my generosity only reaches so far." Severine paused long enough to touch his shoulder and ask, "Are you going to be all right for a few minutes?"

He nodded, and Severine went back inside to find poor Mrs. Grantley curled in on herself on the steps. She sat two steps down from the top and had wrapped herself in a thick fur coat. Mrs. Grantley's shoulders were slumped in and her eyes weren't so much afraid as they were just—damaged.

"It wasn't your husband," Severine told her.

"I never really thought it was."

Severine didn't argue, and she didn't have an opinion. But she had to admit that the woman had brought up the idea of her dead husband so often that she must have—at the least—desperately wanted to.

"You need to leave here," Severine told her. "I'll get your things."

"I'm not leaving," Mrs. Grantley said fiercely. "I won't be driven out of my home."

Severine paused after only one step up and considered. Finally she said, "I can't make you stay gone, but I won't let you stay here alone tonight, and I am not staying with you."

Mrs. Grantley's gaze narrowed with a harsh hatred, and Severine didn't blame her in the least. No woman wanted to be forced from her home by people she barely liked.

"This isn't safe," Severine told her. "Someone is tormenting you."

"I'm not dead yet," Mrs. Grantley hissed.

"The yet is my concern," Severine said. "I'll get you some things to wear."

"I don't want to go," Mrs. Grantley told Severine. "I want to lay in my own bed where I birthed my children and where my husband died."

Severine shuddered, barely hiding her reaction from Mrs. Grantley. Severine paused long enough to consider and then tried gently, "Are you really going to give up now?"

"Give up?" The accusation in Mrs. Grantley's tone was harsh.

"Give up," Severine said firmly. "Curl up into a ball in your bed and wait until death comes for you."

"That's not what staying does."

"It is if you just stay here alone and weak. Go to a hotel, get some rest for a few days, have a massage. Recover your sense of life and then we will face it again."

"We will?" Mrs. Grantley slowly pushed to her feet,

and Severine wondered if she'd have to catch her. The widow swayed and then let Severine lead the way down the hall. Severine found a suitcase in the top of Mrs. Grantley's closet and packed for the woman.

"No! Don't fold it like that. Where is Janice?"

"Is Janice your servant?" Severine asked as she continued to place the same nightgown into the suitcase without adjusting it.

"Yes. Call her. She can do this better than you will."

"She's been given something that is making her sleep," Severine replied. "I'm sure she'd have come to your aid otherwise."

Severine pulled the first three dresses out of the closet that she found and glanced over to see the look of disgust on Mrs. Grantley's face.

"She's probably intoxicated. You'd think it would be harder to get gin for these poor types, but she's either nipping at my bottles or drinking the stuff that'll make you blind."

"Or," Severine suggested, "the health syrup she has next to her bed has been tampered with."

Mrs. Grantley didn't seem to be appeased, and Severine ignored her to cross to the bathroom and find her brush and mirror along with soaps and lotions. She packed the cosmetics and then crossed to Mrs. Grantley, who had thrown out the contents of the suitcase and had slowly started to roll her silk stockings.

"You had three invaders," Severine told the woman, shoving the clothes back in with even less care. "Mr. Thorne has been attacked, your servant was drugged. If they went for reinforcements, we're at a disadvantage. We're leaving. Now. Put on shoes."

"I can't leave like this."

"Your coat covers everything. Add stockings and shoes. You'll be fine." Severine's tone made it clear that Mrs. Grantley would be removed from the premises without further argument. Mrs. Grantley disappeared into her bathroom and when she returned, Severine saw the woman had added a dress. As long as she came without further argument, Severine didn't care. She wrote a quick note for the servant since poor Janice wasn't the primary target and would most likely sleep for hours.

Severine carried the suitcase down the stairs with her free hand on Mrs. Grantley's arm to prevent her from stopping. When they reached the front door, Mrs. Grantley was crying as she locked it. Severine calmly handed over her handkerchief and then stopped by Mr. Thorne. He pushed himself to his feet, and Severine saw a look of pain on his face as he moved.

She placed the suitcase on the ground and said, "I'll get the car."

"I can do it," he said, but she shot him an impatient look and went on her own for the auto hidden in the trees, though Anubis followed after. She struggled to get the car out of the ground that had softened some with dew, but a moment later she stopped in front of Mrs. Grantley's house. She opened the door for Mr. Thorne, and he joined Anubis in the back.

Mrs. Grantley stared at Severine, apparently shocked that Severine had seen to the injured man first. Rather than make a comment, Severine walked round the car, opened the door for the old woman, and waited until Mrs. Grantley had pulled her feet into the vehicle before shutting the door again. She stashed the suitcase in the trunk and drove them back into the city proper.

Despite Mr. Thorne's silent pain, Severine rid them of

Mrs. Grantley at a hotel before asking him, "Did you want to call a doctor or go to their office?"

With his eyes closed, Grayson said, "It's cracked ribs. I've had them before."

Severine lifted a brow and then aimed the car towards their houses. Since he lived with Mr. Oliver and Mr. Brand across the street from her, she'd get him settled, hand him a few aspirin and call the doctor for him.

She drove through the streets of the city slowly, exhausted by the evening. She would have slipped easily into sleep if not for the worry over Mr. Thorne, Lisette, and Mr. Brand. Where were they? Were they safe?

To keep from worrying, she considered what she'd learned about her father in the months since her brother had turned on her. Lukas DuNoir had known something was wrong, something dangerous. He'd moved his family to the country, made singular arrangements for Severine through his apparently only trusted friend, and then only weeks after he'd made those arrangements, he had died.

Had Mr. Brand been Father's only trusted friend, though? Or was he just the one chosen? Father had two brothers, why not one of them? That had been the plan, Severine knew, before she'd learned about the final will. She'd found those earlier dated wills. Severine would have been raised by Florette's parents.

Severine shuddered at the idea. She'd never have been loved and taught by her nuns. Instead she'd have been shuttled between girls' schools and her aunt and uncle's home, always the lesser child. The unwanted extra even as an heiress.

Maybe Father had realized what it would have been like for her. Maybe it hadn't been lack of trust that had engineered the change. But no, Severine thought. No, of course not. Any reasonable person would look to trusted family first to take care of their child.

She took in a deep breath as she parked the car before Mr. Brand's house. Thankfully, she saw that Mr. Brand had returned as well, and she ran up the steps to see if anyone would answer. There wasn't one, so she darted across the street, Anubis at her heels.

She knocked on her own door and called out, "It's me."

The sound of locks turning filled the next seconds and a moment later, she faced Mr. Brand with Lisette and Mr. Oliver just behind. She didn't miss the gun in Mr. Oliver's hand or Lisette's hands on Persephone's and Kali's collars.

To their worried looks, Severine said, "Mr. Thorne thinks he has cracked ribs. I think we should call a doctor. He's still in the car."

Mr. Brand blinked, taking in the news with that one movement. "Are you all right?"

He tugged her inside and she nodded. "Maybe a little bruised."

Mr. Oliver moved past her, jogging across the street.

"You should help them," Severine told Mr. Brand, but seeing the need on his face to ensure she was unharmed, she added, "I'm fine. I promise. Nothing is necessary more than a hot bath and some time to think. Also, Mr. Thorne might need something to help with the pain and at least to have his ribs bound."

Lisette said, "Go. I'll take care of her."

"Lock the door behind me," Mr. Brand ordered.

Mr. Brand disappeared a moment later and the two friends eyed each other. Finally, Lisette said, "We gave chase, but they lost us. They knew the roads well. We didn't. In fact, it took a bit of time to even find our way back here. When you weren't here yet, I barely kept Mr. Brand from going back for you."

Severine started to nod, but a harsh yawn overtook her. She had to shake it off before she could focus again, and her exhaustion was evident in her voice. "There were three of them."

"We only saw two," Lisette said. "And there were only two in the car we followed."

"Then we left one behind with the drugged servant," Severine said. She closed her eyes. "Should we ask the police officers to go check on her?"

"If they drugged her," Lisette suggested, "they probably meant her no harm. She, at least, isn't really involved in this."

"We hope," Severine said, knowing she was too tired to return to that house. She'd have to trust that the married couple at the end of the driveway would look after Janice if anything worse occurred.

"Did you learn anything other than the number of people involved?" Lisette asked.

"Well, clearly the haunting is fake. We'd have known that even if I hadn't found their little headquarters."

"Where was it?"

"In an unused servant's bedroom. I doubt anyone has been in those unused ones for years."

Lisette frowned and then her head tilted. "How did you know there were three if one was at the car?"

"I found three coffee cups. Maybe there's more than three. But there's at least three. And one is a woman." At Lisette's silent question, Severine added, "Lipstick on the cup."

"They were making themselves at home there, weren't they?" Lisette muttered.

"That house is big enough and has so few full-time servants, someone could probably live on the premises and those who are supposed to be there would never know."

"Oh," Lisette shuddered. "Can you imagine?"

CHAPTER 15

*S*everine woke feeling as though someone had wrung her out. She was certainly not used to spending all night out, let alone tossing and turning as she worried about Mr. Thorne and Janice. When Severine finally slipped into sleep, she slept so hard and then, woke in pain from the bruises she gained throwing herself around the house that previous night.

She staggered to her bathroom and considered the tub for a long moment. When she examined herself, she found quite a large bruise on her hip and bicep from when she'd avoided the truncheon, and then matching bruises on the opposite hip and her thigh from the time she avoided the person outside of Janice's room.

Severine wrapped herself in her kimono and went down the back stairs of her house with the dogs following behind. She let them into the garden and turned to face Chantae. Lisette's mother looked Severine up and down and then said, "Coffee."

It wasn't a question, and Severine took it happily, closing her eyes as she sipped it.

"The doctor confirmed Mr. Thorne has cracked ribs," Chantae told her. "I brought the boys breakfast earlier, but they were all still sleeping."

Severine's voice was hoarse and cracked as she said, "Thank you." She rubbed her eyes with the back of her hand. "What time is it?"

"Two, cher."

Severine leaned back with surprise. "Is Lisette up?"

Chantae nodded and eyed Severine with an expression that said she was spoiled. Severine didn't deny it. She had certainly become spoiled. Severine let the dogs back into the house, refilled her café au lait, kissed Chantae's cheek, and made her way back up to her bedroom. She started the bath water, adding salts for her aches and pains and then slid in without letting go of her coffee. A moment later there was a knock on her bedroom door.

Severine called, "I'm in the bath."

"I don't care, cher," Lisette replied. "I'll just lay down on the end of your bed. I visited the boys this morning. Mr. Thorne is up and gritting his teeth heroically while he swears he's ready to engage in the next round of investigation."

Severine was too tired to do anything other than grunt, hoped Lisette heard the grunt, and sipped the rest of her coffee. When she finished drinking her coffee and soaking her bruises, she dressed quickly in a gray plaid skirt that reached her calves with a white blouse and black sweater. The day was gray outside and it matched both her mood, her aches, and her outfit.

"I feel like a personification of gray rain clouds," Severine told Lisette after she'd dressed. "When I finally fell asleep, I had terrible dreams about Janice. I need to check on her."

Lisette nodded immediately. "Mr. Brand asked us to let you sleep, but he thinks we should return to the Grantley mansion and see if we can find what the true intent of this haunting has been."

Severine scratched her brow as she thought about it. "I would suggest we visit Mrs. Grantley to get her permission, but my head pain and body aches say that I wouldn't be the type of person I want to be."

"Why do you care what Mrs. Grantley thinks of your behavior?"

"I don't," Severine admitted. "What concerns me is being who I want to be. I find that I don't have a lot of kindness in me at the moment."

Lisette rolled her eyes. "Cher, cher, cher," she laughed, "you dreamed about a woman you had never met because you were worried about her. You're full of kindness."

Severine adjusted her hair under a turban, so she could embrace the look Meline had created without having to deal with her hair floating around her face. She turned and faced Lisette. "Perhaps you see me and my motivations more kindly because you're my friend."

"Perhaps," Lisette countered, "you don't give your kindness the credit it deserves."

"I am only helping Mrs. Grantley because I want something. Am I kind? Or am I only working for my own ends?"

"Do you care that you pay me even though you call me your friend?"

Severine shook her head. She needed Lisette, and Lisette needed an income. Being the one who provided that income in order to receive Lisette's help didn't change the fact that her friend stood at Severine's side, and made Severine's need to know what happened to her parents a priority. Severine might as well hire Lisette — the one person who had helped her when she didn't have to.

"Let's go visit the woman's house and see what we can find. We'll even bring food and aspirin for poor, drugged Janice," Lisette said brightly.

Severine and Lisette found the gents waiting for them in the dining room. Chantae glanced Severine over and said, "You look like death. You must eat, cher. Your mama and papa wouldn't want you to drive yourself into the grave."

There was something about those words and being in this house that seemed to make their ghosts rise. Was she being melodramatic because she was rather tired? Or was it seeing the coming end of Mrs. Grantley, a woman who had potentially lived like her father had lived? Would he have been so haunted if he'd known he was facing his grave? But maybe he had known he was facing his grave. Maybe he had been haunted too? Maybe the weight of his possible crimes had driven him half mad just as Mrs. Grantley's seemed to be driving her mad?

Severine was seated by Mr. Brand, then her gaze moved to Mr. Oliver, who looked tired, and Mr. Thorne, who had a rather large bruise on his chin, a fat lip, and was very carefully not moving. He hadn't even stood when she and Lisette entered even though his manners were normally impeccable.

"Mr. Thorne, did the doctor give you something for your pain?"

He nodded, jaw clenched. Severine ignored his pride and happily partook of the cheese grits, bacon, and biscuits that Chantae made. They ate in silence and then Severine suggested, "Perhaps forcing Mrs. Grantley to leave last night was a mistake."

"What do you mean?" Mr. Oliver asked.

"Maybe that was their purpose? To get her out of the house? To make her look like she's fleeing ghosts like a hysterical woman." Severine rolled her eyes at the idea and then added, "Or because they wanted access to the house."

"Why didn't they drug Mrs. Grantley too?" Lisette asked. "Then the old women would have slept through whatever they wanted to do."

Severine nodded. "It doesn't make sense to haunt an old woman other than to torment her. Could she have enemies that are that furious with her? You'd think anyone who hated her that much would simply kill her and get it over with."

"Get it over with?" Mr. Brand asked and then coughed into his napkin until tears appeared at the corner of his eyes. When he stopped cough-laughing, he added, "You make it seem as though it were a task like checking something off a list."

Severine fiddled with her grits. "I rather think of it that way. Like a revenge plot fulfilled, and now time to move on."

"I think those who would pursue revenge, true revenge, might find the longer suffering of a person means more to them than one deadly blow." Mr. Oliver cleared his throat and then added with a choked voice, "I would seek the long, slow, agonizing suffering of the person who persuaded my Jane away from those who loved her. I would want the pain to be slow and constant. Like it has been for Gray and I."

As a group, they paused at the stark, unexpected honesty.

Osiris Oliver cleared his throat and his eyes were shining. "I should have trusted you with my purpose and let Gray trust you as well. For that I apologize. I can't...I don't...it's too hard to talk about. I'll—" He cleared his throat. "I'll try to do so. Soon."

"We would like to help," Severine said softly. "When you're ready."

He nodded and cleared his throat once again before draining his coffee. It was a move to hide his emotions and they turned as one back to their plates to give him the space he needed.

They might have over-prepared to go to the Grantley home. Each of them was armed, and even though Chantae was staying home, they armed her as well. This time, they wouldn't be caught by surprise in the dark with the other fellow having a truncheon. Each of them had a flashlight and they brought their own food and drink given what had happened to Janice. They all had sturdy shoes that would allow for the searching of the outbuildings along with the grounds.

"You're staying here, old man," Mr. Oliver told Grayson flatly before they left. "I won't hear an argument. I don't think we should leave this house unwatched, and you're the man for the job. You and one of the dogs anyway."

Grayson didn't argue, which told Severine he was aching and honest enough with himself to know that searching Mrs. Grantley's house for evidence was beyond him. Instead, they turned him over to Chantae and her mother, who had taken up a place by the fire in the kitchen.

The rest of them piled into two autos again so they could separate if needed. This time, Mr. Brand drove Severine while Mr. Oliver drove Lisette. They each had a dog with them and reliable Anubis was lying in the back seat. On the way to the mansion, Mr. Brand glanced at Severine several times without saying a word.

Finally she said, "Speak your mind, Mr. Brand."

He glanced at her and then back at the road. After a long moment that felt like forever, he said, "I liked your father, Sev. He was charming, he was energetic, he was interested in the people who appealed to him. I was one of those people, so—" Mr. Brand trailed off and Severine waited for him to finish.

She could guess what he was going to say, but he was going to have to say it. He was going to have to lay it out because, she suspected, both of them were trying to avoid hurting the other one's feelings.

"I think he was a villain, Sev. I think he was the kind of man who took advantage of the weak. I know he was, in fact, but I made excuses for him because I cared about him. He was always kind to me, and I hate that that is the best I can say of him."

Severine watched the city roll by and then the countryside as they reached the edge of the Grantley property. She took a deep breath. "I know, Mr. Brand. I'm not expecting to discover he was a good man. I just need to know why he and Mother were killed. I don't know how I can proceed with my life without having context for that moment."

He glanced at her again and then turned his eyes to the long driveway towards the Grantley mansion. "That moment?"

"The one where I saw them dead. Dying? Maybe if I'd

run to him and knelt at his side and held his hand, he'd have been yet alive. Maybe I'd have given him a chance to tell me goodbye."

Mr. Brand was shaking his head, but it wasn't the facts of that moment that mattered. Had there been time? The doubt wouldn't leave her. Sister Bernadette had told Severine that her father had likely died within moments. She had said he hadn't suffered long. She had said that Flora DuNoir had died knowing Father cared enough to throw himself in front of her.

The facts weren't enough. That haunting image wasn't going to be exorcised until she had context for why. Villain or not, Severine needed to understand the why of it.

"You don't have to tell me he didn't suffer. Or that I'm wrong about what would have happened if I hadn't frozen at the sight of their bodies. The wondering doesn't go away. The guilt can't just be shaken off. And I knew, even then, that he wasn't a good man. It didn't affect my love for him. Not in the least."

Mr. Brand stopped the car and told her gently, "I'm sorry."

"So am I."

CHAPTER 16

The front door opened when they arrived and an older couple exited. The couple watched the two cars park and then those inside get out. The butler glanced at his wife and they spoke low to each other and then turned back to Severine and the others with emotionless, unwelcoming expressions.

"Hello," Severine said, recognizing the butler. She assumed the woman in the simple black dress was his wife.

"Miss DuNoir," the man said, glancing behind him at his wife. Severine could see that he was nervous, and she had to wonder what was causing his anxiety.

"We've come to check on Janice," Severine started and then trailed off when the man began shaking his head.

He spoke low, as if it were a secret. "Janice woke, read your note, and left this morning. She said Mrs. Grantley would make the incident out to be her fault."

"Do you disagree?" Severine asked curiously.

He shook his head and his wife snapped her mouth

closed with the attitude of a woman who was staying out of it. There was something in her expression, however, but before Severine could ask, she turned and walked silently back into the house.

"We're here to see if we can discover the perpetrator's purpose," Severine told the man.

He glanced back again, and this time, Severine realized he wasn't looking at his wife, but into the Grantley house. Were they not alone? Why was he looking over his shoulder so nervously?

"Are you all right?" Severine asked him with a look at the others to see if they were seeing what she was seeing.

To her surprise, Mr. Oliver had disappeared. She frowned and then caught Lisette's eyes that moved to the side just slowly enough to silently tell Severine where he'd gone. Surely the servants would have seen him leave. Unless…Severine saw that Lisette was standing near the driver's side of the auto and realized that she had left Mr. Oliver and then driven herself the rest of the way.

Severine focused on the butler when he didn't answer. "Why are you looking behind you?"

"Your goal might be easier than you imagined," he answered cryptically, "but I fear that the missus and I won't be able to help you long."

"Why?" Severine asked.

"Janice isn't wrong about Mrs. Grantley's likely reaction. I fear that my wife and I are in the same situation."

"Did something else happen?" Mr. Brand asked.

"While Janice was still sleeping and after you took Mrs. Grantley away, the house was…rifled."

"Shoo," Lisette muttered low.

"What do you mean?" Mr. Brand asked.

"Cabinets are overturned, books are off shelves, paintings have been taken off the walls, someone even broke into the safe. We interrupted them when we arrived and we were locked into a room. We didn't dare to escape until the noises had stopped. Then we tried to call for help, but they cut the phone lines. We don't have a car, and they slit the tires on Mrs. Grantley's."

"Did you see who it was?" Mr. Brand demanded.

The butler shook his head and added, "I saw nothing. They had something on their faces. Stockings, perhaps. All I noticed of one was that he was tall, very strong, and dark-skinned. There was at least one that I didn't see."

"Could there have been three?" Severine asked.

"I don't know. Mrs. Grantley—we've worked for her for a long time, but I think we might have just lost whatever she'd have left us in her will."

His frown was deep and Severine could see that his fears were certainly real.

"What would it have been?" she asked. "Money? Heirlooms?"

"I don't know. She's never said."

"Did you know my father?"

He nodded.

"I'll make it right, but I need your help."

"Make it right?"

"I'll give you a reasonable retirement if you help us through the next few days."

His eyes widened. "I would work for it, miss."

"You will be," Mr. Brand told the man. "I'm Charles Brand, her guardian. Miss DuNoir is generous and kind."

"I don't feel right about taking charity."

"Then work for me," Mr. Brand replied. "We'll give Mrs. Grantley a chance, shall we? If she fails you, I could use the help."

The butler slowly nodded. He was trembling as the stress of the day faded in the light of hope.

Lisette stepped forward and offered, "Let me make you a cup of coffee, shall I? It must have been a terrifying morning."

They went inside together and Severine gasped. The house had been destroyed. Cushions were tossed and ripped open, cabinets were opened, drawers had been emptied. Severine walked through the house that had been pristine the day before and saw evidence of someone destroying everything to find something.

Severine slowly moved through the house, going all the way up to the attics—which hadn't been neglected— and then walked through the first floor again. This time she went into every room and carefully looked for any sign that the people who had done this had found what they wanted.

When she reached what had certainly been Mr. Grantley's office, she sat behind his desk. If she were an old Southern gentleman with this mansion and had something to hide, where would she put it?

Her father had hidden his things in a secondary, secret office. Surely that had to be common for people with something to hide? Did Mr. Grantley have something to hide? She leaned back in his leather chair and stared around the office. Her father's had been lined with books, but it didn't look like Mr. Grantley had been much of a reader or even given to the illusion of one.

There was but one shelf and it looked to have contained accounting logbooks. They were strewn across the office, but whatever had been sought hadn't been those. Severine's father had used just the same logbooks, she thought. She crossed to them and picked one up.

Yes, she realized. Both in the big mansion far outside of the city along with the office in the New Orleans mansion, he had used these similar books. In fact, she thought, he'd used the same ones in his hidden office. The ones that were nearly incomprehensible.

This one, however, wasn't incomprehensible in the least. She flipped through the pages and found entries for paying servants, buying an automobile, and a quite large order of wine and whiskey before the prohibition went into effect.

Unsurprising things. She frowned and guessed that those who had searched this house were looking for the surprising things. She began putting the accounting books onto the shelf. As she worked, her head tilted, catching sight of an object she had seen before.

One of those locks from the master smith. It was hidden in the dark of the shelf just as the one in her father's house had been hidden. Severine ran her fingers over it and knew it for what it was. Mr. Grantley and Lukas DuNoir had used the same brilliant locksmith. Did they have the same secrets to conceal?

She needed the name of that smith. She needed to see if he were bribable. Surely anyone who had made the lock could get through it?

Severine left the office, certain she had found what the criminals had been looking for. Mr. Oliver appeared at the end of the hall, put a finger over his lips, and led the way up the stairs. He opened the door and Severine stepped into the room.

When she started to speak, he shook his head.

She frowned, and he took her hand in an unusually familiar way, leading her across the nursery to a small room where the nursemaid must have once lived. The room held three dresses and cosmetics scattered across a small dresser. There was even money on the top of the dresser.

They slipped from the room and went all the way outside where they could be sure they weren't being listened to.

"What in the world?" Severine whispered.

"I know," he said. "I asked the couple a few times if they had any overnight servants other than Janice. I hit the idea from every side without coming out and asking if they knew someone was living in the nursery."

"Nothing?"

"Nothing."

"So, when she rushed past me last night, she disappeared to the corner she'd taken for herself."

"Very possibly." Mr. Oliver glanced around the property and then asked, "What did the couple say?"

"The servant who had been drugged fled. She expects Mrs. Grantley to hold her responsible, so she packed her bags and walked away from the house this morning. The couple thinks the same will happen to them, but they didn't leave."

"I spied on them for a few minutes," Oliver replied. "The woman limps. I saw the car had been disabled."

"The phone line cut too," Severine added. "They're trapped if they can't walk away."

Mr. Oliver rubbed the back of his neck. "We need to notify the local authorities. Given that one of the criminals is in the house, I think we had better leave. We're at risk if we split up, and we have no idea what they're looking for."

Severine stepped in front of him, so she was facing

away from the house. She met his gaze and mouthed, "I found it, I think."

"Excuse me?"

"I think I found what they need, and I think we should take the couple, leave, and tell the authorities. Mrs. Grantley can hire a guard if she likes."

"We certainly aren't doing it," Mr. Oliver told Severine. "I know you want to find out more about your father, but she's either going to answer your questions or she isn't. We can't put ourselves at risk. They might have left to get sledgehammers and guns."

"Agreed," Severine said. "Are you all right? If Mrs. Grantley truly knows something about your wife—"

"Her long-term servants are afraid of her, Severine," Mr. Oliver said with an almost broken exhaustion. "We can't trust her. We just can't."

"Why don't we help the butler and his wife leave and get resettled and then visit with Mrs. Grantley?"

Mr. Oliver's eyes crinkled. "I'll let you do that part, shall I?"

Severine laughed even though it wasn't all that funny. Mrs. Grantley, even asking for help, was proving difficult to handle. Telling the woman they'd bullied out of her house that it had been tossed? Severine winced for herself and then muttered something about a very nice glass of wine that evening along with several aspirin.

Mr. Oliver laughed. "I see why Gray likes you."

Severine didn't know what to say to that. She knew she blushed, so she shrugged to cover it and said, "Let's gather everyone up before gangsters or whoever is behind this madness return."

She looked up at the house. From the outside, it was lovely. It had wide porches, big windows, beautiful lines.

There were pillars that drew the eye to the double front doors that were works of art in and of themselves.

"Did you grow up in a place like this?" she asked Mr. Oliver.

He shook his head. "We weren't poor, but I wasn't rich like Grayson's family. We had a townhouse in London. My father worked daily. I met Grayson at school and through him, I met Jane. They're higher class than me. Jane never cared. Her parents didn't care. Gray didn't. I was always family and even though I wasn't—" He shook his head. "I wasn't rich. It never mattered."

Severine reached out and took his arm, squeezing the crook of his elbow as though she could somehow provide comfort. They weren't things you could just comfort away. 'It'll be all right' was often a lie. Sometimes, the pain became easier to bear through familiarity and that was the best that could be hoped for.

She dared to ask, "Is she dead?"

Mr. Oliver looked surprised that Severine didn't know. Slowly, painfully, he said, "I don't know."

CHAPTER 17

Severine met Mrs. Grantley's gaze after the woman wound down from screeching.

"This is all your fault," the old woman accused.

"The discovery that you had someone living in your home? Yes, I suppose we were able to discover that for you."

Mrs. Grantley's eyes narrowed and she hissed, "Get out."

Severine rose. They were in the dining room of the hotel, and she thought that this was a moment that needed to end in beignets, café au lait, and possibly wine as well. Her head was pounding but before she left she said, "We've made steps to help you. If you want more help, you'll need to give us something far more concrete than a woman's name who may or may not be bribable."

When Severine stepped back into the lobby, Mr. Brand rose. He lifted a brow in inquiry, but Severine had reached the point of paranoia where she feared eavesdroppers. A man brought their car around and as Mr. Brand seated her in it, she caught the sight of the tall man with the scar, Landon Gentry.

When Mr. Brand sat next to her, Severine nodded towards the man and Mr. Brand cursed. He started to leave the car, but she grabbed his arm. "Don't. He's letting us see him on purpose."

As Mr. Brand pulled onto the street, Severine caught a glimpse of familiar faces. Her cousin Florette, Grandmère, and Severine's half-brother, Andre. Severine kept her eyes on them, but only Andre noticed her going by in the vehicle. He nodded with a smirk. He had wanted to be seen, too.

Florette was chatting animatedly and Andre leaned towards her. Was she imagining the connection between the two? Or was her paranoia just growing? Severine pressed her hands to her temples and then asked Mr. Brand, "Did you see them?"

"I did."

"And I told you about my suggestion to Flora?"

"You did," Mr. Brand agreed. "You wonder if she can be trusted now?"

Severine nodded, rubbing her chest. She would never have wondered this at the nunnery. It was her family that had driven her to this level of suspicion. She couldn't be more grateful to have been given over to the nuns. Severine shook her head and then leaned back, letting her head rest against the seat.

"Don't make her your most trusted confidant." Mr. Brand glanced at her and then tried, "But she's also young and far less free than yourself. She can't just do whatever she wants like you can."

Severine admitted that she had already concluded that Florette would never be a close confidant. She just hadn't expected to see Florette flirting with Andre.

"We need beignets," Severine declared.

Mr. Brand turned right and parked in front of a beignet shop moments later. She stayed in the car while he ran in and got enough beignets for all of them. The paper bags he brought back to the car smelled like oil and powdered sugar, and her mouth was watering the entire way back to her house.

"I've been thinking," she said as they found themselves once again around the table.

No one said anything as they fiddled with their beignets, coffee, and red wine.

Severine took a bite of the lovely pastry, unapologetically showering herself with powdered sugar. Then she grinned, closing her eyes to savor it, before continuing. "My father's big house had a secret office and the Grantley house has a secret also, locked by that same master locksmith."

"Yes." Grayson's pained look had increased since they'd left him earlier that day, and if the way he squinted at the lights were any indication, his headache matched her own.

"What if this mansion has the same?"

Mr. Brand cleared his throat and Lisette breathed, "Cher—"

Severine popped two aspirin into her mouth and drank them down with her sip of wine. She handed her bottle of aspirin to Grayson and he took it with an expression of relief.

"Where would it be?" Lisette asked.

Severine shook her head and confessed, "I don't want to look for it yet. I just want to eat too many beignets, have a second glass of wine, take a second bath, and then curl up in front of a fire and fall asleep re-reading the scene where Mr. Rochester confesses his love for Jane Eyre and everything is happy. I want to fall asleep before things go awry and dream about a happily ever after instead."

Lisette's mouth dropped open. "Have you just had those few sips of wine?"

"It's the exhaustion speaking," Severine admitted without an ounce of shame. "I'm useless when I'm extremely tired. It hits me out of the blue and then I get giddy, which is followed by weepy. The key to life," Severine confessed as though she were conveying a great secret, "is to never get caught out when you cross the line to weepy."

Mr. Brand snorted on laughter and Severine grinned at him unrepentantly, finished her beignet, and took both her wine and the nearly empty bottle. "Good night, dear loves. Mr. Rochester and I have an appointment."

She left to the sound of their subdued laughter and found her way to her room. Her bath was just long enough to relax her hips again and then she crawled out of the water and into her bed. As much as she wanted to curl up with her book, she was asleep before she even picked it up.

THE PROBLEM with falling asleep so late that it was already morning, meant getting up without enough sleep, and then collapsing into your bed mid-evening. Then, having gone to bed so early, waking before the sun had risen, and the entire house still sleeping.

Even the dogs refused to leave her bedroom. Anubis lifted his head and then dropped it again, as if to say she needed to get back into bed herself, and he would set the right example. She yawned deeply and then took herself down to the kitchens to make coffee.

She almost dozed off making the coffee and then cursed her betraying body that had just earlier refused to go back to sleep. Once she finished making the coffee, she filled a larger farmer's-type mug. It was one like the workmen used and not something normally found in the cupboard of a spoiled heiress. She took her milky coffee and escaped into the library. She paused at the library doorway and found that all of the books had been slipped from the shelves.

She lifted a brow, guessing that her friends had searched without her the previous night. It hadn't been destroyed like Mrs. Grantley's home, and the dogs had rested easy, so they hadn't been invaded. Severine checked each shelf of the library and found that they'd been unsuccessful thus far.

The two hidden locks had been in bookshelves, and it had informed their search the previous evening while she had slept. What about her father's actual office? The hidden locks had also been in the offices of the house. Severine left the library and found her way down the hall, opening the door to her father's old office. Her friends hadn't forgotten where the locks had been found, judging by the piles of books to either side of the shelves just inside the doorway.

Severine sat in her father's seat and looked up. A part of her remembered sitting just there, across the desk. Her father had read the letter from the headmistress at her school while she watched, nibbling her bottom lip. She had known that it wouldn't be bad; she wasn't a problematic child. And yet, she'd shifted and squirmed waiting for the look of disappointment on his face.

Had he seen that in her? He must have, she thought. He, an experienced man. Her, a child. Of course he'd seen her worry. How had he reacted? She couldn't quite remember. Hadn't there been something about her being too quiet in the letter? Well-behaved, but awkward? She felt certain there had been, but she couldn't remember how he'd reacted.

She closed her eyes on the memory so strong, it played out before her like a silent film that cut off too soon. Had he scolded her? Had he disregarded the comments and made a joke? Had he asked a question or two and saved his thoughts? Had he felt as helpless in his pursuits as she did in this one?

Severine would have done much to find Sister Mary Chastity in that moment and talk to her. Her eyes would crinkle with a soft blue edge. She'd say something wise and understanding and Severine would feel that whatever had happened, it would be all right.

She swallowed back the rising emotions and dark thoughts. This is what became of someone who slept odd hours and was pursuing a murderer. Why did what she was doing matter now? She frowned and reached for her coffee.

Severine put her feet up on her father's desk to remind herself she was grown and in charge of her own future and continued to sip from the cup while the sun rose. She pondered recent events and realized that something had changed. More than her returning home. Those hidden offices had been around since before her father died. They had existed in all the years between her father's death and that morning.

"What has changed?"

If she was speaking to her father's ghost, she didn't feel as though she had gone mad. She would have given much to speak to him again. Where had it all gone wrong for him? Had his journey to the suspected villainy been a slow journey of compromises or a decision that said wealth and power mattered more than anything else?

She shook off that thought. It was always followed by the far more haunting question. How did she avoid it? How did she create a better life when she must have the same tendency in her? How did she reconcile the fact that of her two parents, she preferred to identify with the harsh Lukas DuNoir rather than her spoilt, useless, and cruel mother?

Severine stood suddenly and determinedly crossed to the shelves that framed either side of the door. There was nothing on the empty shelves. No hidden lock, no secret passage. Severine examined each of the wooden panels of her father's office. She unlocked the hidden safe and looked again at the contents. There had been jewelry in there when she'd opened it. There had even been a gift purchased by her father for Severine at some future date. There had been a stack of currency. There had been two guns. There had been the deeds to several properties. But there hadn't been an explanation of why he had been murdered.

She shut the safe after taking out the master key that had been made for the big mansion in the country. She sat again, this time opposite her father's seat but a moment later, she moved. The memories were fast, thick, and weighty enough to be ghosts. She closed her eyes and wondered again. How had he reacted to that letter?

She wanted to believe that he'd snorted and muttered about the hysterical ramblings of girls' school mistress, but she was certain that was wrong. Had she hidden in the curtains? She'd done that sometimes. Slipped behind them and stood ever so still. Father would see her disappear and let her do it without a word.

How many times had she heard a snappish comment to Flora because Severine had been hiding and Father hadn't cared that his harsh words affected more than Flora?

Severine rose and traced the unseen path of her younger self to those curtains. She slipped behind them as easily as she had then. Thin and tall, it wasn't so hard for her to hide herself in the thick velvet folds.

She leaned back, pressing the back of her head against the wall.

Don't let it bother you, Sevie.

Severine flinched at the words. The memory was so strong, so clear. And, she thought, so false.

Miss Mannigan, is she the one with the hair slicked back against her head? The painful looking bun and the brown dress?

Yes, Severine thought. Yes, that bit was real. She could hear it again. She felt it again. As though her younger self had made her way out of her soul and possessed her body once again. The years of love from the sisters were gone in that moment. The pain of losing her parents. The fear of being an orphan and unloved. The terrifying journey to a country where she didn't speak the language. All of that fell away and all that was left was her younger self. The simple Severine who wanted her father to tell her everything would be all right.

Yes, Papa. Severine had answered his question without a delay. Yes, Miss Mannigan was the severe one. The other girls had teased Severine often that she already looked like the pinched-mouth spinster.

Do you want to be like her when you grow up, Sevie?

No, Papa.

A grunt next, she thought. A grunt and nothing. Severine closed her eyes. How she'd ached over that sound. What had it meant? Did he hate her too? Did he think it was too late? Did he see her in her schoolteacher?

Mama had entered then, Severine remembered.

Lukas, did you read it?

Of course I did.

What are we supposed to do with her? She's a hobgoblin.

Severine closed her eyes then and she did now too. She rubbed her chest and she remembered Father's answer.

As long as she isn't like you, Flora. Get out.

Severine had remained unmoving then. This time she stepped out of the curtains, eyes still closed. Her hand was on her chest as she crossed to the mirror and examined her face. She'd slept with her hair tied up with rags to provide the loose curls. There were dark circles under her eyes, and her mouth was tight. Her eyes were too big, too dark, too wide, and too filled with old pain. She could image Flora over her shoulder, looking with dissatisfaction at her daughter in the mirror.

Before another memory attacked Severine, she fled the office, chased by the truth: she hadn't mourned Flora DuNoir. Severine hadn't been sad when her mother died. And, she hadn't forgiven Flora for the years between Severine's birth and Flora's death.

CHAPTER 18

She ran up the stairs and dressed, chased by the ghost of her mother. To block the sound of her voice, she harassed the dogs out of their beds and out to the garden. The fresh air didn't help. Another cup of coffee along with aspirin didn't help. Stretching her muscles tightened by bruises and horrible memories didn't help.

Severine ran back up the stairs and examined her closet. How dour was she when every dress was black, gray, wine red, and dark blue? Severine dug through it all, rejected it all, found the boxes from Meline and found a rose dress. When Severine put the pale pink dress on, she looked in the mirror. She didn't look like anything other than the child she had been, dressed up in frills that never made her pretty. Severine stripped the dress off and threw it to the side.

She leaned over, hands on her knees and took deep breaths. Kali licked Severine's leg and Persephone whined. Anubis, however, watched Severine with dark, loving eyes.

"It's not my fault," Severine told the dog. "It's not my fault that I have dark hair and eyes. It's not my fault that I'm not effusive and shallow. It's not my fault that she didn't love me."

Anubis huffed and then flopped down, his gaze on her.

"She didn't love anyone," Severine added, "not even herself."

Persephone whined again, and Severine picked up a black day dress. It was sleeveless, cut to her body, and made her look like the lush, exotic version of a bright young thing. She added cosmetics, taking special care to put them on as she liked them rather than how Mother had worn them.

She finished with the long strand of Tahitian pearls that Father had purchased for her. A white gold tag hung from the clasp, and it had been engraved, For my dark flower, Sevie. As she finished dressing, she refused to think of anything other than where a hidden cache could be.

As Severine finished with her shoes, another memory struck her. Father had once had the master suite redone while Severine had been at school. In the process, the location of the closets had changed, and Flora had complained bitterly about a smaller space but Father had only mocked her.

Severine rose. Her memories had assaulted her far more deeply than the bruises she'd attained, but she crossed to the master suite, into her father's closet, shoving aside clothes that no one had bothered to remove.

There, at the back of his closet, was the lock. She pulled the key from her bodice and unlocked it.

Nothing happened. She frowned and threw his clothes aside. She tried the key again, but no. It was right. She had unlocked it. Severine put her hands on the wood-paneled wall and tried to shove. They didn't fold in, but there was the barest of movements. Severine ran her fingers over the panels again, cursing the lack of light in the closet.

She moved by feel and found it then. The seam in the wood paneling that had edged apart the slightest bit. She gasped and dug her nails into that seam and pulled. The panels rolled back easily but she was entirely unable to see anything.

Severine ran down the stairs and found a lightbulb. Chantae had risen and was making eggs, bacon, and biscuits in the kitchen while Chantae's mother kneaded bread at the counter.

"Good morning," Severine called as she grabbed the lightbulb and darted back up the stairs, chased by Anubis. Severine grabbed a wooden chair from the hallway and dragged it into Father's over-sized closet. She hopped onto the chair and struggled to replace the lightbulb. After long enough to be shameful, light filled the closet, and Severine gaped.

On the floor were the remains of her father's wardrobe. The wood paneling from the floor to her waist were just as you would expect. At halfway up the wall, however, the closet paneling rolled back to show a compartment that was, perhaps, four feet wide, three feet tall and no more than a foot deep. The compartment was lined with shelves.

This was not what had her gaping. Massive stacks of currency were hidden behind the panels. At least three stacks of green bills bound with rubber bands. She lifted just one bundle off of the first stack and flipped through it, seeing hundred dollar bills. Severine had no doubt that this money wasn't earned in a decent manner.

She pressed her hand against her chest and then closed the closet door.

"Anubis, ruhig."

The command to be silent was followed by one to guard.

"Anubis, beschützen."

His gaze focused on her, and his alert eyes ranged the small space while his ears perked in concentration. She lifted a quite heavy burlap sack and found three gold bricks. Her mouth dropped open, and she took the accounting books, a stack of letters tied together, and a small black notebook. How many times had she seen that very notebook or one like it in her father's pocket?

Severine took the books with shaking hands, sick to her stomach, and carefully closed the panels, locked them, replaced her father's clothes in front of the panel. And then for good measure, she replaced the good bulb with the burnt out one, using one of her father's cravats to unscrew the hot bulb.

She changed the overhead light of her father's bedroom. Father had a safe in his bedroom that had been empty for some time. Severine frowned deeply as she placed the books inside it and then replaced the painting over the safe.

As she returned the wooden chair to the hallway, Lisette stepped out of her own room.

"Morning, sunshine," Lisette said cheerily. "Feeling better?"

Severine silently nodded and then hated herself as she

asked, "Doesn't that smell good?" She didn't like the fear that drove her to keep her secret from her friends.

"Bacon and eggs always smells good, cher," Lisette replied. Her gaze moved over Severine's face. "Are you all right? You look pale under that rouge."

Severine rubbed her brow as she said truthfully, "Bad memories and a headache. I just remembered that Father had a safe in his room. I found some letters, two of those impossible-to-read accounting books like Grantley had, and a notebook Father used to carry."

Lisette gasped. Her wide smile and bright eyes made Severine feel like the world's worst friend, especially when Lisette asked, "Have you read anything yet?"

"I left it in the safe," Severine said, not lying at that moment and yet feeling as though she were succumbing to the devil to hide anything from Lisette, who had been nothing but helpful. "I thought it might be better to pretend we know nothing in case your old friend is still watching us."

Lisette's brows lifted and Severine quickly added, "Also, I know I'm not thinking very clearly and I thought I'd better eat and return to myself before I made any bigger choices. It's like…every step I take deeper into this mystery makes me feel like I should hate him."

"It's all right that you don't hate your father, Sev. He was your father and from the few things you've said, the only one who was kind to you until Brand and the nuns showed up."

"I would give up a fortune to speak to them today," Severine said.

Lisette reached out gently. "Perhaps you'd find some comfort speaking to a priest?"

Severine paused, considering, and finally confessed

her fear. "I feel like I'll become like my parents if I'm not careful."

"They weren't inherently bad," Lisette told her as they left the hallway and made their way down to the dining room. They'd already been invaded by the gents next door, so Lisette whispered before they joined them. "You aren't bad, Sev. And you'll continue to avoid such a fate every time you make a choice to be kind, to do good instead of evil, to—excuse me while I channel my granny here—but sow peace rather than discord."

Severine nodded because there was nothing else to do, and then they joined the others.

MR. BRAND WAS FIXED on Severine with a steadiness that told her he didn't believe one bit of her story. Not while they ate the breakfast Chantae made. Not while they returned the books to the shelves in the library. Not when Thorne and Oliver left to hire several private detectives. Mr. Brand didn't believe Severine's story when Lisette went to help her grandmother in her bedroom.

Severine met his gaze, and he met hers.

"You saw inside the bedroom safe already?" she guessed.

"I cleaned it out after your parents died." They looked at each other for long minutes and then Mr. Brand said, "You don't have to tell me."

"It wasn't good."

"So I gathered."

"I'm not ready."

He nodded. "When you are, I'm here for you, Sev."

She tried to smile, but she couldn't quite do it. Instead

she nodded again. "What did he do? That saved your life? That made you friends?"

Mr. Brand met her eyes. "He had come to visit where I was stationed during the war. I was young, useless, and stupid. We were attacked, and I should have died, but he shoved me out of the way."

"So you lived?"

"I lived, but I was pretty badly hurt. I got sent home, and he saw me through college when I should have been dead. Then he gave me a job. I would have done anything for him. Anything, Severine. But all he asked of me was to protect his daughter if he could not."

Severine wished her heart were touched, but it wasn't. There had been too many bad memories that morning. Too much pain before she'd found all that evidence of her father's villainy. Normal people didn't have coded accounting books and stacks of money. Good people didn't. Normal, good people weren't murdered at a house party.

Normal, good people didn't need to ask near-strangers to look after their child because no one close to them was trustworthy. Normal, good people didn't live the life Lukas DuNoir had lived, and even though she hadn't committed any of his crimes, she felt as though she was carrying the burden of all his sins.

"I don't know how to be his daughter."

"It isn't a thing you do any particular way, Severine." Mr. Brand's gentle voice was not comforting.

She rubbed her dog's head and ears and wished that she didn't feel a darkness in her chest. Slowly she breathed in. "Do you know what Sister Mary Chastity told me was the most important?"

He shook his head.

"Kindness."

He just waited.

Severine explained, "'Thou shalt love the Lord thy God with all thy heart, and with all thy soul, and with all thy mind. This is the first and great commandment.' I told her I didn't know if I believed in God."

"Don't you?"

Severine shrugged, playing with the cross that she'd put on underneath her dress. She pulled it out and held it, looking down at the emblem of the son of God's death rather than explaining her conflicted feelings. Her belief and her lack thereof. Her desire to shake her fist at the heavens and demand why her, while knowing she had been so very lucky.

Severine ignored all of that and answered, "She promised me that God would give me the time to come to know Him. In the meantime, she said, 'Thou shalt love thy neighbor as thyself.' Then she suggested kindness."

"Kindness is a good choice, Severine."

It was a good choice, but was it enough?

CHAPTER 19

"What if we use one of those private investigators to follow Landon Gentry?"

Lisette gasped but it was her mother, Chantae, who said, "That's a good way to get a man killed."

Severine blinked. "Killed?"

"Landon wasn't a good boy, and he is a worse man. If I'm ever struck down, it was him who killed me, and I was a second mother to him when he was a boy," Chantae said firmly. "My girl loved him, and I was stupid enough to hope that he'd be better."

"He never was," Mr. Brand finished.

Both Chantae and Lisette nodded.

"What if we approach Cocotte again?" Severine suggested.

"She's not going to say a word if Landon Gentry saw you leaving her." Chantae was the one who answered again while Lisette silently traced her finger over the table. "Cocotte lands on her feet. As long as Landon has his gaze on her, she'll never speak or help."

"I could offer more money."

"You can't spend money if you're dead," Chantae replied, ruining that idea before it could do more than pass from Severine's mouth to the grave.

"The question," Severine said, rubbing her brow to soothe the headache she couldn't quite shake, "is what changed?"

"What do you mean, cher?" Chantae asked as Severine ran her cross along its chain.

"I mean that my father has been dead for years. So has Antoine Grantley. Why are they bothering his widow now? What are they looking for? Why is this Gentry fellow focused on me when he shouldn't even know who I am? Surely it can't have anything to do with me?"

"It could be the questions I've been asking since you've been home," Mr. Brand said with the same exhaustion Severine felt. "Or it could be something else. Something that is separate from you, but you matter now."

"Like what?" Lisette demanded.

"Well." Mr. Brand cleared his throat. "There's every evidence that supposedly upstanding men like Lukas DuNoir and Antoine Grantley were part of a conspiracy. Perhaps it is as simple as a break in leadership."

"So it doesn't have anything to do with Severine? But Andre—" Lisette began.

"Yes, but when did Andre end up under that man's thumb? Recently or years ago? We don't really know, do we?"

Severine's head tilted as she considered. "If Andre has been this person's man for a while, it has more to do with his connections than with me. Or me alone."

"It wouldn't be you, though, Severine," Lisette said. "It would be your father. Perhaps they tried something with

Mr. Brand, failed, and then turned their attention to Andre because he was the next closest man to your father. Someone who might have access to the hidden office at the big mansion or the safe here."

Severine ignored the stab of guilt at the evidence of her lie and focused on the last bit. Outside of herself and Andre, who else would have had a chance at the hiding places Severine had found since returning to New Orleans?

She glanced at the others. "They all seem to be quite wealthy regardless of whatever else was happening. What if they weren't looking specifically for money?"

"Then they were still looking for something valuable," Mr. Brand guessed. "Something that money couldn't buy."

"Something," Severine started to say, priceless, but for the sort of insanely rich people like her father, priceless things were status symbols. Expensive collections were intended to show that he'd reached a level of money that outstripped others, but they all had their little things. The jewel that had supposedly once belonged to Napoleon. Art stolen during the war and then purchased illegally. Hidden vaults of paintings. One of her father's types might fight over things like that, but when they failed to acquire the newest symbol, they pursued another.

"Something that you can't buy because the other owned it."

The others weren't following her idea.

"Not something like a house. Houses are a dime a dozen if you're rich, but we think whoever is behind this was in some sort of illegal conspiracy, correct?"

"It seems likely."

"Where?" Severine suddenly demanded. "They used

the Spirit Society to pass messages and the like, but surely they weren't committing crimes through notes alone?"

Mr. Brand's brows lifted. "You mean like a speakeasy?"

"Something that you can't just steal away. Something that you can't buy yourself. What if, at least part of it, is a membership roster? Evidence of criminal activity that can't just be sloughed off."

"You know," Mr. Brand said, "I read about a person who was making gin. They knew they were being watched, but they couldn't just move the business. It was too much to hide. In trying to do so, they were uncovered."

"A property," Severine suggested quickly. "Something that you can't walk away with. Something that would be on record, so you could claim it."

"A deed of ownership," Mr. Brand nodded. "If they were making something or using a location for transporting or filtering smuggled goods, it might be nigh impossible for the others to switch locations."

"And," Severine said, "if I or the somewhat repentant Mrs. Grantley had the deed of ownership, they might lose everything."

"They might," Mr. Brand finished, "even be arrested, depending on the activity."

"If whoever behind this is rich like Mr. DuNoir," Lisette said. "For all we know, Landon Gentry's thug employer realized that there's a stash of something valuable in the home where only weak women live, like with Mrs. Grantley."

Before they could discuss the possibilities further, Mr. Thorne and Mr. Oliver returned. They brought with them pale and frantic expressions.

"What happened?" Severine demanded.

"We got a letter from Madame Cocotte."

"You didn't speak with her?"

Mr. Thorne shook his head. "It was a name, an address, and a picture of my sister just outside of that address. If the date on the back of the photograph is to be believed, it was taken after we thought she died."

Severine gasped and then Mr. Brand said, "That's awfully interesting timing."

Mr. Thorne looked at Mr. Oliver and they both nodded.

"Is the address far away?"

Mr. Thorne nodded, his gaze avoiding hers.

"You have to go," she told him without rancor. "Jane is why you're here. She might need you."

Mr. Oliver cleared his throat and he met their gazes. "It's probably a trap. They want us out of the way."

Severine thought the same, but she wouldn't pile onto their problems with her own. Their sister and wife deserved their help more than Severine and her friends.

"If they want you out of the way," Mr. Brand said, "we have to expect that they're trying to weaken us."

"It doesn't matter," Severine said. "Jane Oliver is their priority and she might be alive. We can't...I won't ask them to sacrifice that for us."

"I can't not go," Osiris Oliver said simply. "I can't take that chance."

"I agree with Severine," Lisette said. "You must go."

Mr. Brand said nothing, but his gaze was focused hard on the table, and then he said, "Severine is right. The living, or potentially living, come before the dead."

"You all are living," Grayson Thorne snapped. "You are living, and we do care about our promise."

"Then you stay," Mr. Brand suggested. "Have Oliver go

after his wife, and you stay. We'll make them think you're gone, and we'll arm you to the teeth and keep you out of sight."

"They'll try for the dogs," Mr. Oliver said suddenly. "They have no idea what things Grayson and I have acquired in our time looking for Jane. We have enough to put pause on any attack if they were to attack you directly."

"I think we can expect a cross of subterfuge and stronger measures," Severine said. "Though who knows?"

"How far away is the address?"

"At least three days if we went, found nothing and immediately returned."

"They'll expect you to try all avenues," Mr. Brand said. "We'll have to hide Thorne inside the house and make it seem as though he went."

"And," Severine added, "every person who comes to the house will be a suspect."

"In, say a week?" Lisette shook her head. "We'll have your cousins, your aunt, your grandmother, various daily maids who've come a half-dozen times before. We'll be wide open."

"No," Severine said, "because we'll never let up on our guard."

"And," Mr. Brand added, "we'll make you quite ill. The moment Mr. Oliver leaves, Severine will come down with a terrible flu. We'll use her headaches. She's had them often enough."

Severine's eyes widened. "No one knows they're not from something else."

"If we aren't leaving, they can't weaken us outside." Mr. Brand rubbed the back of his neck and then rose to pace back and forth.

It was Lisette who paused and demanded, "Do we actually think we'll be attacked?"

Everyone looked at each other and then Chantae said, "They may well think they'll be able to do the same thing they did to that servant couple. Burst in, wave around a weapon, and lock you in a bedroom while they search for whatever they're looking for."

"I feel paranoid and mad," Severine announced, not having to pretend to have a headache.

"This is mad," Mr. Thorne told her with gentleness that she wasn't sure she deserved, liar that she was. "But so is my sister disappearing. So is haunting an old woman. So is the murder of your parents along with the murder of Antoine Grantley. We aren't dealing with people who make rational choices."

"Who are we dealing with, then?" Lisette muttered.

Her mother answered for them all. "Devils with the face of upstanding men about town. You're dealing with those who chose power and gain over everything else. Those aren't the type of men to lock you into a room and rifle through your things. They're the type of men to murder their host and his wife with hundreds of other well-connected people around. They're fearless and evil. We need to be careful. They may well block the door and set the place on fire."

CHAPTER 20

It took three days for Florette to arrive at the New Orleans mansion. When she arrived, Severine ran to the back of the house and up the stairs and threw herself into bed. A few minutes later, Florette came into the bedroom with Chantae, who was carrying tea instead of café au lait.

"I have chamomile for you, cher," Chantae said. "Try to drink some."

Severine turned onto her side and rubbed her brow. She tried to avoid being dramatic about rubbing her brow but attempted to convey that her head was hurting. She slowly pushed up to a sitting position and Florette leapt to her feet, shoving pillows behind Severine's back.

Florette's voice was a whisper when she said, "Headache? Pain?"

Severine nodded.

"Grandmère said your mother used to have those, too."

Severine didn't want to talk about Flora DuNoir, so a subject change was in immediate order. Her voice was a little too fake when she asked, "Did you persuade them to let you live with Grandmère?"

Florette nodded happily. "Grandmère bought immediately into helping me. I was able to get up and dress and Grandmère said I should come check on you and then I left the house alone."

Florette's vibrant blush said that Grandmère had said something entirely different. Severine nodded weakly and sipped the tea. Would it have been so hard to make chamomile and mint for this scenario? Chamomile alone was both boring and gross.

"Andre—" Florette blushed prettily this time, but her gaze avoided Severine.

"My brother who shot me, yes," Severine replied and then rubbed her shoulder as though it still pained her.

Florette bit down on her bottom lip. "He's been attentive."

Severine met Florette's gaze. "I won't tell you pretty lies, Florette. Not about Mr. Oliver or about Andre. My brother is a villain, and you are beautiful, rich, and well-connected."

Florette met Severine's gaze with an unexpectedly stark honesty. "Yes, I know. But he makes me feel better about Mr. Oliver and everything."

"So you'll forget he's a villain?"

"No," Florette said and then added, "but I'm vain enough to like the attention."

"Just don't fall in love with the lies. I'm sure he's quite convincing."

Florette shook her head. "Once you see his nastiness, you can't not see it. He's mean all the time. But he tells me I'm pretty and he brings me chocolates and flowers, and I like those things."

Severine closed her eyes against the idiocy of it all. Florette was nearly half a year older than Severine, and it seemed that Florette was still a child. Or maybe, Severine thought, Florette was a normal young woman, and it was Severine who had aged beyond her years.

"Just remember that Grandmère is Andre's first defender. If she has to choose between your happiness and his, she'll choose him every time."

Florette nodded, but Severine didn't believe that Florette truly thought that applied to her.

Severine changed the subject again or she'd have been forced to lecture Florette further. "Andre, what? What were you going to say?"

Florette flushed. "He saw Mr. Oliver and Mr. Thorne leaving."

Severine stilled, and if she weren't pretending to be ill, she'd have sat up, spine straight, and then leaned in for more information. Andre had been watching their house? Severine examined Florette for signs of guile, some sign that she knew she'd been sent for information.

"Yes, I believe so. I was already in bed at that point. Lisette mentioned a short trip."

"Do you know where they went?" Florette asked and it took a moment for Severine to revel in the idea that it was Florette who was leaning in excitedly.

"Just family business. I didn't really pay attention." Severine finished her lie with a long sip of tea and met Florette's gaze around her teacup.

There was awareness in those pretty blue eyes. There was guilt in the light blush on her cheeks. Severine pretended she didn't see it and leaned back. "I'm sorry, Florette. I need to lie down again. My head—" Her voice was weak and dramatic, and Severine wasn't going to continue this charade.

Florette had found out what the ones who sent her wanted to know. Yes, Mr. Oliver and Mr. Thorne had left town. They had packed their bags, driven far outside of the city in a field where one could see for quite a distance and unloaded Mr. Thorne's bags into Mr. Brand's car.

Mr. Brand had then brought Mr. Thorne back to the city, smuggled him into the DuNoir mansion, and he was just across the hall.

"WELL?" Lisette asked as Severine exchanged her pajamas for a day dress and met her friend's gaze in the mirror.

"She found what she was seeking."

Lisette winced. "You don't know she's their creature."

Severine nodded and then parted her hair in the middle, severely creating a bun at the base of her neck. "Do I look like a hobgoblin?"

Lisette stared, having no idea what drove the question. "You look a bit serious. Like you're ready to face a potential house-breaker as Mrs. Grantley's servants did. No time for hair in your face, but Severine—" Lisette's eyes moved over her face and she gently asked, "You do know you're quite beautiful, don't you?"

Severine smiled as if she believed Lisette, but given the look on her friend's face, she didn't think she sold it. Instead of replying to that bit of nonsense, she asked, "Do you know that you saved me? I don't know what I would have done to come here, having left behind all those I loved, and only found the monsters that are the DuNoirs and their associates. It seems you only need one ray of light in an otherwise benighted world."

Lisette laughed and they found their way back down the stairs for lobster rolls and bouillabaisse. Severine possibly indulged in a cocktail on the sheer joy of the name—Angel Tears—and then stopped after one cocktail, so she wasn't drowning her sorrows with gin and fruit liqueur.

One full day later, after another boring afternoon brightened only by another Angel Tears, there was a knock on the door. The air of the room shifted from bored to oppressive. Mr. Brand met Severine's gaze and then moved to Mr. Thorne. The two men nodded at each other and Mr. Thorne patted his pocket where a heavy iron weight lay.

Mr. Brand rose. He crossed to the door and opened it. They all leaned forward to listen and heard a surprised, "Ms. Grantley?"

Severine relaxed and then gasped when she heard a thump and the dogs all sat up, ears forward. Anubis let out a low growl and she gasped.

"Mr. Brand?" Lisette called.

"Hide," Severine told Mr. Thorne. "They aren't looking for you."

"I'm not here to hide," he told her.

"I know," she hissed back. "But if they overpowered Mr. Brand, they can overpower you. Be sneaky."

He frowned and then slipped out the side entrance to the dining room and, she guessed, directly into the silver closet. He was just in time as Landon Gentry, Andre, and Amelia Grantley entered the house.

"Your poor grandmother," Severine said to Amelia, who flushed.

"We asked her to come live with us time after time," Amelia hissed.

"Is your father Philip?"

Amelia paused and Severine could see it was true. Philip, the probable murderer of his own father. There was something on Amelia's face that told Severine the woman didn't know why the name of her father was significant but she nodded. Severine wasn't surprised.

"I can see that your grandmother was kinder to you than you were to her."

Amelia waved a gun and Andre ordered, "Quiet, Sevie."

"The hidden office was in the tunnel at the big mansion," Severine told him. Her brother responded by reaching out and slapping her hard. Her head snapped to the side and her cheek pulsed with pain. She could taste blood in her mouth, but she turned and met his gaze without a sound.

Anubis growled, and Severine grabbed his collar, holding him to her side.

"He had one here too." Andre eyed Landon and Amelia, ignoring the bristling dogs as he said, "We'll lock them in a room and search."

"Where?" Amelia demanded. Her eyes never touched Severine, as if she didn't want to see what happened next.

"Upstairs," Andre ordered. "The rest of the hidden spaces have been on the bottom floor."

Landon grabbed Lisette's arm in one hand and Chantae's in another. Severine went ahead of the man without trouble or comment, calling her dogs. Their good behavior was the only reason her brother hadn't shot them, she knew. That and the sound it would make.

She wouldn't risk them. She walked up the stairs and entered her father's bedroom silently. Lisette and Chantae followed and Landon locked them in a moment later. He eyed them all, scoffed darkly, and said, "You should have just come."

The statement was dark enough and mean enough that it conveyed another message. They weren't supposed to live through this. Why lock them in the room? Severine voiced the question a moment later and Chantae answered, "Probably the girl. I bet she thinks she didn't sign on for murder."

"They'll do what they want, kill us, lock her in before she can object, and then she'll be their creature."

"Do you think the mastermind is this Philip Grantley fellow?" Chantae asked.

"If we survive," Severine answered, "I would like to find that out."

"Granny—" Lisette murmured, her eyes on the ceiling. The elderly woman had disappeared up to her bedroom to nap after lunch. Would she be all right?

Severine closed her eyes and prayed with her whole heart, hoping that someone was listening. When she opened her eyes, she gasped. All three dogs were eyeing the window and a moment later it was pushed open and Grayson tumbled into the room.

Severine rushed to help him, guessing his ribs were aching once again.

"They've bound Brand to a chair," he said. His green eyes were alight with fury, and he added, "Andre is in the office. The girl is searching the library. The big one is watching the front door."

Severine looked at the others. "I lied to you."

All gazes landed on her. She decided to show them rather than to explain. She crossed to the closet, pushed the dusty clothes aside, unlocked the door with the key she'd added to her cross chain just the day before. She moved the panels and then stepped back so the light from the bedroom windows could show the panels.

"Oh my heavens," Chantae breathed.

"There's no way this is the cache of a man who isn't a criminal," Lisette told Severine with her usual blunt honesty.

"I know. It's why I didn't want to show you. I am full of shame."

"This isn't you," Grayson told her. "None of us think that. And now—" He grinned and took the rifle case. In moments, he'd cleaned and loaded the gun, handing Severine his own. "I know you won't hold back."

"I shot the ground, not him."

"We still need to get out of here," Lisette pointed out. She took the next cleaned and loaded gun from the cache.

"I can do that," Severine replied, locking the panel and replacing the clothes. She took the key from the lock and crossed to the bedroom door, and easily unlocked it from the other side. "You'd think that Andre would have remembered Father and his love of master keys."

"Who cares about that?" Lisette demanded. "Mama, go for granny. I'll try to get Mr. Brand free."

Severine and Grayson eyed each other and he said, "Clearly, I'll handle your brother."

CHAPTER 21

Severine had learned to be quiet when she spent time in the woods outside the nunnery. You didn't get to see birds and fawns if you cracked branches. She was silent on the stairs with Grayson just as quiet behind her. There was a part of her that wanted to ask him if he was naturally quiet, but instead she slipped into the kitchen. Lisette had headed up the stairs with her mother first, gun at the ready.

She met Grayson's gaze and separated from him. He went first, heading towards the library while she slipped inside the open door of the office.

Amelia Grantley was the perfect young woman. With her golden hair and ready smile, she had been exactly what Severine's own mother dreamed of. She moved with grace as she dumped the books off the shelves and searched for a hidden lock.

Severine placed the gun against the back of Amelia's head with casual ease and the girl froze.

"I told Landon he should have tied you up," Amelia said.

"Into the closet," Severine ordered.

"You aren't a criminal." Amelia turned and eyed Severine. "You were raised by nuns."

"Into the closet," Severine repeated.

Amelia smiled. "To be feared, you have to be believable." A breath later she shouted, "They're loose!"

Severine's eyes widened in surprise and then she heard a shot. She pressed the gun against Amelia's chest. "You had better hope I didn't just lose a friend," Severine told her and then heard another shot and shouting.

Severine stepped back, lifted her gun, and brought it down hard against Amelia's head. She crumpled and Severine took a moment to tie Amelia's hands behind her back. She then darted to the corner of the room just as her brother threw the door of the office open. He stepped only far enough into the room to take in the sight of Amelia, then shouted, "Sevie!"

Of course she didn't answer. A moment later she heard pounding on the steps and guessed that Landon was searching up the stairs.

Hide, Lisette, hide.

Severine heard loud cries from Chantae and Granny and then there was another thump and the sound of breaking glass.

"Was that your little black friend, Sevie?" Andre called in a sing-song. The gun in his hand arrested her. "Is she dying just now? Bleeding and alone, regretting helping you?"

Severine adjusted her grip on her gun and wondered if she'd be able to shoot her brother. Would she be able to strike him down? Her earliest memories included him.

They weren't necessarily good memories, but they were hers and they had defined her. Didn't Sister Sophie say that being your brother's keeper meant more than people realized? You looked after those who God gave you. You took care of them. You made sure they were all right.

You didn't shoot them.

"Sevie!" her brother sing-songed again and then there was another clatter from near the front of the house. She gathered her courage as she heard Mr. Brand call, "I've got you in my sights, Andre. I'll shoot you and I won't lose sleep over it."

"Sure you will, servant." Andre sounded so smug. "Do you know who I am? Do you know that this town will crucify you for messing with one of its chosen sons?"

Severine moved slowly. She could see his smug face through the crack in the door. He held his hands out in mock surrender, but she could see the finger moving on the gun.

"Are you a chosen son?" Severine asked, stepping out and lifting her gun to aim it at her brother.

Their gazes met. She with her father's eyes. He with their mother's eyes. Years seemed to flash between them. Time after time of discord. Moment after moment of shared history. Pain that belonged to them both and divided them.

"Sevie, you won't shoot me."

She cocked the revolver without a word.

"I've got this, Sev," Mr. Brand told her with worry. "This isn't your burden. It's mine."

"Shooting your brother will ruin you, Sevie," Andre said with complete confidence. "The self-righteous acolyte of a slew of nuns. Do you know why your father chose that nunnery, Sev?"

"I do," Severine answered without hesitation.

He grinned evilly, ignoring her answer, and she knew he'd revel in whatever would come out of his mouth next.

To stop what he would say, she told him, "I'm not under the illusion that Lukas DuNoir was anything but a villain."

She could see actual surprise in her brother's expression and then he spun, shooting at Mr. Brand. Severine shot at her brother, but she closed her eyes as she did, and she missed. He shouted a laugh and ran down the hall and towards the back door.

Severine rushed to Mr. Brand, but he was sitting up. "I'm fine. Grayson is bleeding."

"Charles," Severine said, using Mr. Brand's first name for the first time, even as she rushed to Grayson. "I closed my eyes. I didn't want to shoot Andre."

"He's gone," Mr. Brand replied. "That's all that matters."

Mr. Thorne was holding his hand to his side, trying to stop his bleeding. He was pale and she dropped to her knees, pushing him onto his back so she could put pressure on his wound.

"Lisette?" Mr. Brand called.

"He escaped through a window," Lisette answered down the stairs. "Mama is hurt."

Mr. Brand ran up the stairs and came down with Chantae.

"We need a doctor," Severine said and then noticed the howling of her dogs, locked in the bedroom upstairs.

"I'll use the phone across the street," Lisette said and ran out of the house.

～

THEODOSIA GRANTLEY HAD SEEMED QUITE old when Severine had spoken with her at that party so long ago. The widow looked like the walking dead as she took in the sight of her granddaughter bound to a chair and gagged in the office of Severine's house. Mr. Oliver stood over her, having just returned from his fruitless hunt.

"What do I have to do to handle this myself?" Mrs. Grantley asked. "What is the price for my granddaughter?"

Mr. Oliver cleared his throat, glancing at Severine with a plea. She nodded as he said, "We want real answers."

"I can give you names and places," Theodosia Grantley said. "I shall need a pen and a paper."

They waited in silence as she scratched out the words. The sound of the pen moving across the paper was the only sound in the whole of the house. Mr. Oliver watched each movement of the pen with desperation. Mr. Grayson, pale from blood loss, watched with exhaustion that said he'd given up hope. Mr. Brand watched with disgust, knowing that there would be no real repercussion for Amelia Grantley.

Severine didn't watch the old woman. She eyed Amelia, who returned her look with hatred. That was fine. Severine didn't think much of her either. The silence was broken by hammering and Severine glanced towards the front of the house where Lisette was supervising the addition of iron bars on the windows of the house. The locks had already been replaced and a new door had been added.

They had been invaded once and Severine was going to make sure it didn't happen again. When the list was handed to Mr. Brand and Mr. Oliver, they read their papers and then Mr. Brand nodded at Severine to cut the ropes on Amelia Grantley.

She slowly rose and started to say something, but Mrs. Grantley snapped, "Silence."

And with that, they left the room and the house.

"Is this where we celebrate victory?" She was exhausted. "I don't think that's what this was."

"We won this battle," Mr. Brand said.

"And we'll win the war as well," Mr. Thorne added.

"And then?" Severine asked. "What comes after this?"

It was Granny who answered from the doorway. "Good days and bad. Happiness and sadness. Perhaps a long summer by the sea with quiet. And some of that kindness your nun ordered up. Kindness fills the heart after days like these."

"What shall we do that is kind?" Severine asked, entirely without an idea.

Granny immediately answered with the most unexpected of words, "The DuNoir Free School and Home for Girls."

It was just the right thing to say. Suddenly, like the parting of clouds to let through the rays of the sun, hope danced through their hearts.

The END

Hello friends! Thank you for giving this new series a chance. I so hope you enjoyed Severine's beginning, the introduction of Brand, Thorne, Oliver, Lisette, and others. A review for this book would be so very helpful. If you would be willing, please leave a review.

. . .

As TIME GOES BY, the mystery of Severine's past and her parents death will be uncovered. In the process, we'll also discover more about why Thorne and Oliver are in Louisiana rather than England and what is driving their own investigation. Along with that, we will uncover a little more about Lisette and her family. I hope you're as excited as I am to dive into these bigger mysteries.

THE SEQUEL to this book is now available.

October 1925

The hunt for the person who killed Severine's parents continues, and things are intensifying. She's finally got a direction to discover just what her parents had been doing? Will she be able to find out why they were killed?

As she presses forward, she again encounters the man in

the shadows. Who is this person who is trying to stop her from learning more about what was happening when her parents died? Why is he invested enough to find her expendable? And just what will happen if she continues?

Order yours here.

If you enjoy historical mysteries, you may enjoy, *Death by the Book*, the first in a completed series.

Inspired by classic fiction and Miss Buncle's Book. Death by the Book questions what happens when you throw a murder into idyllic small town England.

July 1936

. . .

WHEN GEORGETTE DOROTHY MARSH'S dividends fall along with the banks, she decides to write a book. Her only hope is to bring her account out of overdraft and possibly buy some hens. The problem is that she has so little imagination she uses her neighbors for inspiration.

She little expects anyone to realize what she's done. So when *Chronicles of Harper's Bend* becomes a bestseller, her neighbors are questing to find out just who this "Joe Johns" is and punish him.

Things escalate beyond what anyone would imagine when one of her prominent characters turns up dead. It seems that the fictional end Georgette had written for the character spurred a real-life murder. Now to find the killer before it is discovered who the author is and she becomes the next victim.

KEEP on flipping to read the first chapter or order your copy here.

SNEAK PEEK OF DEATH BY THE BOOK

GEORGETTE MARSH

Georgette Dorothy Marsh stared at the statement from her bank with a dawning horror. The dividends had been falling, but this…this wasn't livable. She bit down on the inside of her lip and swallowed frantically. *What was she going to do?* Tears were burning in the back of her eyes, and her heart was racing frantically.

There wasn't enough for—for—anything. Not for cream for her tea or resoling her shoes or firewood for the winter. Georgette glanced out the window, remembered it was spring, and realized that something must be done.

Something, but *what?*

"Miss?" Eunice said from the doorway, "the tea at Mrs. Wilkes is this afternoon. You asked me to remind you."

Georgette nodded, frantically trying to hide her tears

from her maid, but the servant had known Georgette since the day of her birth, caring for her from her infancy to the current day.

"What has happened?"

"The…the dividends," Georgette breathed. She didn't have enough air to speak clearly. "The dividends. It's not enough."

Eunice's head cocked as she examined her mistress and then she said, "Something must be done."

"But what?" Georgette asked, biting down on her lip again. *Hard.*

CHARLES AARON

"Uncle?"

Charles Aaron glanced up from the stack of papers on his desk at his nephew some weeks after Georgette Marsh had written her book in a fury of desperation. It was Robert Aaron who had discovered the book, and it was Charles Aaron who would give it life.

Robert had been working at Aaron & Luther Publishing House for a year before Georgette's book appeared in the mail, and he read the slush pile of books that were submitted by new authors before either of the partners stepped in. It was an excellent rewarding work when you found that one book that separated itself from the pile, and Robert got that thrill of excitement every time he found a book that had a touch of *something*. It was the very feeling that had Charles himself pursuing a career in publishing and eventually creating his own firm.

It didn't seem to matter that Charles had his long

history of discovering authors and their books. Famil-iarity had most definitely *not* led to contempt. He was, he had to admit, in love with reading—fiction especially—and the creative mind. He had learned that some of the books he found would speak only to him.

Often, however, some he loved would become best sellers. With the best sellers, Charles felt he was sharing a delightful secret with the world. There was magic in discovering a new writer. A contagious sort of magic that had infected Robert. There was nothing that Charles enjoyed more than hearing someone recommend a book he'd published to another.

"You've found something?"

Robert shrugged, but he also handed the manuscript over a smile right on the edge of his lips and shining eyes that flicked to the manuscript over and over again. "Yes, I think so." He wasn't confident enough yet to feel certain, but Charles had noticed for some time that Robert was getting closer and closer to no longer needing anyone to guide him.

"I'll look it over soon."

It was the end of the day and Charles had a headache building behind his eyes. He always did on the days when he had to deal with the bestseller Thomas Spencer. He was too successful for his own good and expected any publishing company to bend entirely to his will.

Robert watched Charles load the manuscript into his satchel, bouncing just a little before he pulled back and cleared his throat. The boy—man, Charles supposed—smoothed his suit, flashed a grin, and left the office. Leaving for the day wasn't a bad plan. He took his satchel and—as usual—had dinner at his club before retiring to a corner of the room with an overstuffed armchair, an Old-Fashioned, and his pipe.

Charles glanced around the club, noting the other regulars. Most of them were bachelors who found it easier to eat at the club than to employ a cook. Every once in a while there was a family man who'd escaped the house for an evening with the gents, but for the most part —it was bachelors like himself.

When Charles opened the neat pages of 'Joseph Jones's *The Chronicles of Harper's Bend,* he intended to read only a small portion of the book. To get a feel for what Robert had seen and perhaps determine whether it was worth a more thorough look. After a few pages, Charles decided upon just a few more. A few more pages after that, and he left his club to return home and finish the book by his own fire.

It might have been early summer, but they were also in the middle of a ferocious storm. Charles preferred the crackle of fire wherever possible when he read, as well as a good cup of tea. There was no question that the book was well done. There was no question that Charles would be contacting the author and making an offer on the book. *The Chronicles of Harper's Bend* was, in fact, so captivating in its honesty, he couldn't quite decide whether this author loved the small towns of England or despised them. He rather felt it might be both.

Either way, it was quietly sarcastic and so true to the little village that raised Charles Aaron that he felt he might turn the page and discover the old woman who'd lived next door to his parents or the vicar of the church he'd attended as a boy. Charles felt as though he knew the people stepping off the pages.

Yes, Charles thought, yes. This one, he thought, *this*

would be a best seller. Charles could feel it in his bones. He tapped out his pipe into the ashtray. This would be one of those books he looked back on with pride at having been the first to know that this book was the next big thing. Despite the lateness of the hour, Charles approached his bedroom with an energized delight. A letter would be going out in the morning.

GEORGETTE MARSH

It was on the very night that Charles read the *Chronicles* that Miss Georgette Dorothy Marsh paced, once again, in front of her fireplace. The wind whipped through the town of Bard's Crook sending a flurry of leaves swirling around the graves in the small churchyard and then shooing them down to a small lane off of High Street where the elderly Mrs. Henry Parker had been awake for some time. She had woken worried over her grand-daughter who was recovering too slowly from the measles.

The wind rushed through the cottages at the end of the lane, causing the gate at the Wilkes house to rattle. Dr. Wilkes and his wife were curled up together in their bed sharing warmth in the face of the changing weather. A couple much in love, snuggling into their beds on a windy evening was a joy for them both.

The leaves settled into a pile in the corner of the picket fence right at the very last cottage on that lane of Miss Georgette Dorothy Marsh. Throughout most of Bard's Crook, people were sleeping. Their hot water bottles were at the ends of their beds, their blankets were piled high, and they went to bed prepared for another day. The unseasonable chill had more than one household enjoying a warm cup of milk at bedtime, though not Miss Marsh's economizing household.

Miss Marsh, unlike the others, was not asleep. She didn't have a fire as she was quite at the end of her income and every adjustment must be made. If she were going to be honest with herself, and she very much didn't want to be—she was past the end of her income. Her account had become overdraft, her dividends had dried up, and it might be time to recognize that her last-ditch effort of writing a book about her neighbors had not been successful.

She had looked at the lives of folks like Anthony Trollope who both worked and wrote novels and Louisa May Alcott who wrote to relieve the stress of her life and to help bring in financial help. As much as Georgette loved to read, and she did, she loved the idea that somewhere out there an author was using their art to restart their lives. There was a romance to being a writer, but she wondered just how many writers were pragmatic behind the fairytales they crafted. It wasn't, Georgette thought, going to be her story like Louisa May Alcott. Georgette was going to do something else.

"Miss Georgie," Eunice said, "I can hear you. You'll catch something dreadful if you don't sleep." The sound of muttering chased Georgie, who had little doubt Eunice was complaining about catching something dreadful herself.

"I'm sorry, Eunice," Georgie called. "I—" Georgie opened the door to her bedroom and faced the woman. She had worked for Mr. and Mrs. Marsh when Georgie had been born and in all the years of loss and change,

Eunice had never left Georgie. Even now when the economies made them both uncomfortable. "Perhaps—"

"It'll be all right in the end, Miss Georgie. Now to bed with you."

Georgette did not, however, go to bed. Instead, she pulled out her pen and paper and listed all of the things she might do to further economize. They had a kitchen garden already, and it provided the vast majority of what they ate. They did their own mending and did not buy new clothes. They had one goat that they milked and made their own cheese. Though Georgette had to recognize that she rather feared goats. They were, of all creatures, devils. They would just randomly knock one over.

Georgie shivered and refused to consider further goats. Perhaps she could tutor someone? She thought about those she knew and realized that no one in Bard's Crook would hire the quiet Georgette Dorothy Marsh to influence their children. The village's wallflower and cipher? Hardly a legitimate option for any caring parent. Georgette was all too aware of what her neighbors thought of her. She rose again, pacing more quietly as she considered and rejected her options.

Georgie paced until quite late and then sat down with her pen and paper and wondered if she should try again with her writing. Something else. Something with more imagination. She had started her book with fits until she'd landed on practicing writing by describing an episode of her village. It had grown into something more, something beyond Bard's Crook with just conclusions to the lives she saw around her.

When she'd started *The Chronicles of Harper's Bend*, she had been more desperate than desirous of a career in writing. Once again, she recognized that she must do something and she wasn't well-suited to anything but writing. There were no typist jobs in Bard's Crook, no secretarial work. The time when rich men paid for companions for their wives or elderly mothers was over, and the whole of the world was struggling to survive, Georgette included.

She'd thought of going to London for work, but if she left her snug little cottage, she'd have to pay for lodging elsewhere. Georgie sighed into her palm and then went to bed. There was little else to do at that moment. Something, however, must be done.

Order your copy here.

A Murder Most Odd

Nearly A Murder

A Treasured Little Murder

A Cozy Little Murder

Masked Murderer

Meddlesome Madness: A short story collection

Silver Bells & Murder

Murder at Midnight

A Fabulous Little Murder

Murder on the Boardwalk

THE MYSTERIES OF SEVERINE DUNOIR

The Mystery at the Edge of Madness

The Mysterious Point of Deceit

Mystery in the Darkest Shadow

The Wicked Fringe of Mystery

The Lurid Possibility of Murder

The Uncountable Price of Mystery

The Inexorable Tide of Mystery

THE POISON INK MYSTERIES

(This series is complete.)

Death By the Book

Death Witnessed

Death by Blackmail

Death Misconstrued

Deathly Ever After

Death in the Mirror

A Merry Little Death

Death Between the Pages

Death in the Beginning

A Lonely Little Death

(This series is complete.)

Philanderer Gone

Adventurer Gone

Holiday Gone

Aeronaut Gone